a Horse
Brought Us
Here

a novel

DERSHIE M^cDEVITT

Editing, design and, distribution by Bublish

ISBN: 978-1-64704-827-3 (paperback)
ISBN: 978-1-64704-828-0 (e-book)

Out of nowhere,
a horse brought us here
where we taste love until we don't exist again.

—*Rumi*

This novel is dedicated to Brandon,
Trent, and Kendal McDevitt.

chapter one

JUNIPER, WYOMING

Rob Hitchcock was the first boy I let touch my breasts. It happened the spring of our freshman year, long before he was the big-deal quarterback at Juniper High but not before he'd started going steady with my best friend, BJ Bonniface.

My girlfriends and I had piled into Calvin Sharpe's car full of guys at the A&W Drive-In that night when Rob changed places to get in the back seat with me. I still remember the electric feelings that shot through me when he leaned over and started tracing the bare skin across my collarbone with his calloused thumb. "You know what, Nella?" He'd grinned, his husky voice going low. "I have a place I want you to see. I bet you Calvin will loan me his car for an hour." I noticed Rob's sweet-stale smell. He'd never paid attention to me like this. Maybe it was because he was drinking the real beer the Bohingi Boys had gotten, not root beer, like me.

I had a horrible crush on Rob. His eyes were so friendly, his fingers so warm. I smiled back. "Really? Well, okay, Rob. Sure. Ask him."

"You're gonna really like this place." His words slurred a few minutes later when Rob kicked everyone else out of the car and the two of us burned out of the A&W Drive-In onto Main. Rob rolled Calvin's car window down and rested his elbow on the sill, driving with only his right hand. "It won't take us long." But he went clear through Juniper and didn't stop till we got to the end of the deserted road out past the Wyoming Girls' Reform School.

He turned off the car lights, took another drink of beer, and put his arm around me, pointing at a huge yellow moon hanging over Mount Quandary. "Neat, huh?" Then he fiddled with my ponytail and slipped the rubber band off. "I want to see your hair down."

When my hair fell loose to my shoulders, something inside me quivered. He smiled. "Hey, you look real pretty that way." An owl hooted in a tree above us, which gave me goose bumps, but the good kind. I wasn't ready, though, for what happened next.

His muscly arms gathered me in. He took my face into his rough hands, steered my mouth to his, and kissed me hard. Kept on kissing, like he really liked me.

I'd kissed boys before in spin-the-bottle games, but they were nothing like kissing Rob. My conscience was screaming, "Stop this, Nella!" His tongue went into my mouth, and that startled me, his sweet-stale smell something to taste now. Then his hands were under my blouse and inside my bra. I'd never let anything like that happen before. He was so strong it would've been impossible to stop him, but honestly—and this surprised me—I didn't want to. My heart hammered wildly, and a fizzy, funny-bone feeling zigged through me that dissolved all my resistance.

A whole year later, Dad would warn me about Calvin Sharpe's Chevy, with its rebuilt motor and raked rear end:

"Don't ever let me hear about you riding in that car, Nella. It has trouble written all over it." But that night, pressed so tight against Rob on the fuzzy seat cover of Calvin's car, I didn't know enough to worry.

The thing is, I'm actually what people in Juniper call "a nice girl," which matters in a small town like ours, where everybody knows everybody else's business. Nothing more ever happened between Rob and me, but for two and a half years, I prayed he hadn't told BJ about it. It was truly the only secret I'd ever kept from her. Lately, though, I was worried she may have found out. Why else would both she and Rob have been acting so standoffish?

Monday, October 28, 1959

"Nella, help me understand something here." My second-best friend, Midge Mahoney, turned sideways in the passenger seat of my open Jeep as we drove down Main Street on the way to school. "How come guys get to have all the fun?" She was pointing at a drunk Indian man leaning precariously against the paint-peeling door of the Ideal Hotel. The eagle feather in the band of his high-crowned black hat was bent kittywampus over its brim. "Take him, for example." Her eyebrows came together disapprovingly. "He can go in Lu-Lu's, but because we are allegedly innocent girls, we can't! Well, I'm dying to know how a whorehouse actually works." She frowned. "Do you know anybody who's actually been in the Ideal who'd share actual, real details?" She unzipped a plastic pencil holder in her notebook and took out her usual box of Red Hots as I braked for a light.

3

If BJ found out about Rob and me, would Midge know?

Midge opened the box, filled her hand with candy, and poured it in her mouth, talking through the pieces.

How can anyone eat candy at eight o'clock in the morning?

"Where would you start: clothes on or clothes off?" She paused thoughtfully. "And sheets? You'd change them every time, wouldn't you?" She nodded. "You'd have to. With my luck, I'd be assigned the laundry detail."

"What is this?" I stopped at the red light, turned, and stared at her. The same shiny black hair framed the same rosy-cheeked, round face I'd known since first grade at Coffeen School. Jacks; jump ropes; snow angels; Mother, May I; and now Lu-Lu's? "Are you investigating prostitution as some college alternative?"

She threw me a dirty look as I shifted back into high gear. "I just wonder, that's all. Normal human curiosity." Her bangs blew up from her forehead as I sped around the corner off Main and past Mr. Hedley's weathered HONEY 4 SALE sign. "It would take real nerve to be a hooker. Lexie Medina's sister has a friend who knows a guy whose sister is a hooker who got herself in the family way." She paused, tossing more candy into her mouth. "But hookers aren't like ordinary people." She chewed as she talked. "You know, rushing to the altar, then telling everyone their little eight-pound papoose is premature. They've got true remedies and the nerve to use them."

"They do?" Mom's warning rang in my ears: *There is absolutely nothing a girl can do if she gets pregnant, Nella, that doesn't do permanent damage. Men marry virgins, honey. Save yourself for your husband. You'll never be sorry.*

"Yep. Simplest tool in the world to get rid of a baby—a bottle of pop!"

"Nooo."

She smiled. "Honest. It works. I don't mean to get over-graphic or anything, but first you open the bottle. Then put your thumb over the opening. Be sure it's sealed. Then shake up the bubbles and put it up—well, you know, inside. Slide off your finger, and let the bubbles do their work." She drained the Red Hots from her hand into her mouth again. "It'd be sticky as anything and nasty to boot, but still, it's not a bad thing to know about."

"You've got to be kidding. Even if it worked, you could get an infection or do something awful to yourself, Midge."

She licked her lips, then her red fingers. "Probably, there's some risk. For a Catholic like me, it would be a mortal sin, but I know for a fact that Mary Lou Kropowsky's best friend knows a girl it's worked on three separate times."

"Well, I'd never have the nerve to do it." I turned wide onto Shawnee.

"Tell you something else I bet you don't know," Midge said. "Doc Justice goes up to the Ideal every month to test Lu-Lu's girls for VD and gives them penicillin shots if they need them."

Midge's big brothers must tell her this stuff.

"I don't believe you. Everybody knows Sheriff Madsen lets the Ideal stay open to protect girls like us when horny cowboys come to town and get drunk. But Doc isn't going to break another law just because the ban on prostitution isn't enforced."

"You'll believe me this time," Midge crowed, "because BJ's who told me. Plus, she knows the names of actual high school and college guys that go up to Lu-Lu's." She pulled her lipstick out of her purse, put it on pink and thick, and gave me a significant smile, one eyebrow slightly raised.

Midge definitely knows something.

I shifted to slow down at an intersection. "BJ told you?"

BJ didn't tell me.

She and I always discussed things you'd never talk to anybody else about: How to shave your legs. Could you French-kiss with braces on? Were you still a virgin if you used Tampax?

"How could BJ know about Doc, Midge? You don't think Rob told her, do you?"

"Well, duh. Of course I think he did. You go steady with a guy for over two years, you talk to him about"—she lowered her head, batted her eyelashes—"everything."

I shivered.

Then he probably told her what happened in Calvin's car.

Two and a half years after that night in the car, I still felt nervous around Rob. And blushed. Always blushed. Rob was taller now than when we were freshmen—at least six foot three, with curly black hair and hungry dark eyes. No wonder he made me jittery. His muscles crawled under his skin when he barely moved his arm, and he always smelled like Aqua Velva. Sometimes I wondered if I didn't really want it to happen that night in Calvin's car. I just wished Rob had talked to me about it afterward, said something—anything—but he never had.

The bridge over Quandary Creek was bumpy. I gripped the steering wheel tighter, and Midge grabbed the windshield. My predictable Juniper world had gone topsy-turvy since Rusty, the creep, my about-to-be-former steady, had turned out to be a traitor, and BJ was acting more distant every day. I thought your senior year was supposed to be your best year.

"Nella?" Midge's voice was soft. "I wasn't trying to hurt your feelings, kiddo. Honest. You're worried about BJ, aren't you?" Her round eyes looked sorry for me. "This weekend probably didn't help any."

She knew me too well. I realized I was chewing my thumbnail and stopped.

"Don't take it so personally," she said. "If you ask me, BJ's just got a bad case of queen-itis. The big head, if you know what I mean. She even acted weird to the two of us on the court Friday night." Midge gave me a disgusted look. "I'm telling you the truth. I've never seen a grumpier homecoming queen." She patted my arm, her sticky fingers warm and somehow reassuring, and held out the Red Hots box to me. "I've got three left. Take 'em all."

"No, thanks." My voice caught in my throat. "It's like BJ's changed, Midge. Something's different." I took a breath. "For what it's worth, I didn't talk to her all weekend."

"What? Criminy!" Her eyes narrowed. "Nella, what is going on?"

"Yeah. What is?" I downshifted to turn onto Piney Creek Road. The air was cooler there along the creek, and I cut the heater on so at least our feet were warm. Midge was sitting sideways again, her black eyes boring into me.

I wish I knew how much Midge knows.

I tried ignoring her. The bright-yellow pine needles covering the road ahead blurred into gold. I brushed my sweater sleeve over my eyes, hoping she'd miss my tears, but she didn't.

"Okay, Nella. Out with it."

"There's not much to tell, Midge. I called BJ on Saturday and again on Sunday. Her mom took messages both times. BJ just didn't call back." I'd probably feel a lot better if I told Midge the whole story, but if she didn't already know, she could still blab it. Anyway, it hadn't been two days since BJ and I'd talked on the phone; it had been two weeks.

The high, thick limbs on the pine trees along the street came together over our heads, making the road dark and chilly. The smell reminded me of the mountains above the Bar Z, the Bonnifaces' ranch. BJ and I had ridden her Shetland ponies all over those hills when we were kids, slowing down only for a drink from Quandary Creek. BJ had been my bossy teacher in purple earmuffs. "Drink upstream from the cattle. Never drink downstream from the herd."

"Hey, Red!" Henry Sibley, pumping gas at the corner Esso Station, cocked the bill of his cap back like he wanted to see me better, then let out the usual long wolf whistle. "Slow down and marry me." I ignored him like I always did and tucked a strand of hair back in my ponytail.

"Ah, Nella, loosen up. He's one of the few guys in the world that actually looks good in a baseball hat. Give the guy a break."

I've ignored Henry Sibley how many hundred years? And now Midge was even picking on me for that. I felt shaky and unsure of myself. I reached to wipe a spot off the windshield, tried to swallow and couldn't. This was already a cruddy day, and we hadn't even gotten to school yet.

I downshifted into second as we started up the hill to Juniper High. Midge finished her Red Hots, unzipped the pencil holder in her notebook, and put the empty box in it. A *Modern Screen* was wedged there, all ready for study hall.

Her voice dropped to secret-telling. "Wouldn't you just kill to know the whole truth about BJ and Rob?"

"What whole truth?" I slowed to turn in front of Mr. Cooper's little grocery, the rusted metal Coke sign hanging over the door swinging in a gust of sudden wind.

"Geez, make me spell it out! Whether they go all the way—you know, do it. They've been going steady for soooo long."

"You are turning into a pervert, Midge. We've covered this a billion times. You know as well as I do BJ would want to save herself for her husband."

Midge shook her head slowly. "You're actually serious, aren't you?" Her words were kind but somehow condescending. "I used to feel that way, too, you know—about waiting till I got married. In the last year, though, I'm thinking about changing my mind."

I noticed the arrow-pierced heart in blue ink on the front of Midge's notebook: *MM + MC.* "Wait a minute! You're not talking about BJ. You're talking about you and Mike, aren't you?" She'd been dating Mike Chase, this really smooth college guy, since last spring.

She squinted down at her notebook. "Well, he has gotten me thinking. He says some people go through all this agony waiting till they're married and then find out it's not so great together." She began scraping red polish off her thumbnail. "What if that happened, Nella? And anyway, why is it always the girl who's got to say no? I hate that. Boys can do whatever they want to. It's unfair."

I flipped on the radio to buy a little time. Roy Rogers was singing "Happy Trails" on one of Juniper's two equally crummy local stations.

Midge moaned. "Seriously," she said, raising her voice over the radio, "what would you do if you married somebody and then found out it was no good with them? Think of all that wasted time."

Everyone in Juniper doesn't need to hear her.

I cut off the radio.

"There are ways to keep from getting knocked up, Nella. You're not even Catholic, so you could use something besides the rhythm method. Wouldn't you be a little tempted with Rusty if you didn't have to worry about getting pregnant?"

"Not really. Mom says once you get married, that's the time to work things out." Anyway, Rusty, the big-headed senior-class president, was now officially the last guy on earth I'd want to do it with. I hated him! He'd agreed to be Lorna Casey's escort in the homecoming court, when I hadn't even been picked and she and BJ and Midge had.

"It's just that it's a once-in-a-lifetime opportunity," he'd said, staring down at his big gold class ring on the chain around my neck. The creep hadn't even had the guts to look me in the face. That was one thing Midge hadn't noticed this morning—that I wasn't wearing Rusty's ring.

She'd gotten awful quiet all of a sudden. I looked at her sideways. Her arms were folded tight across her chest, and she was staring straight ahead, put out about something. I couldn't think of why or what to say. The silence between us felt heavy. She began drumming her fingers on her notebook, like she couldn't wait to get out of the Jeep and away from me.

I shifted into low for the steepest part of the pull up the hill. Near the top, she stopped the drumming, pulled a pencil out of her purse, and started chewing on it, leaving little beaver marks all up and down its shiny yellow surface. When we reached the top, the sun was warm, and the purple mountains surrounding our valley came into view. Only the peak of Mount Quandary, the highest mountain, was hidden by clouds.

I looked for BJ by the drinking fountain outside the school, where she always waited for us. She wasn't there, but the girls' guidance counselor, Miss Cantor, was. The wind had picked up. She motioned us to the curb with a chubby pink hand, the wind puffing out the back of her rose-colored cardigan. "Nella, Nella, pull over. I need to speak with you at once." The minute I pulled the Jeep to a stop beside her, she said, "Park your car, girls, and come straight to my office," then turned and walked away. Something really had her upset.

By the time we'd parked, Midge had remembered at least six rule infractions Miss Cantor might be about to nail us for. "They've probably already got BJ in the office. Anything deviant we've done was her idea, so don't panic. Keep your mouth shut, and let BJ do the talking, especially if it's about how many times we cut Music Appreciation."

Miss Cantor disappeared through the wide double doors on the brick front of the building as we got out of the Jeep. One corner of a blue-and-gold BEAT CASPER homecoming banner still draped there caught a gust of wind and broke loose. It flapped around and made a snapping noise, like a sheet on a clothesline in an angry wind.

chapter two

"Girls, I wish I could soften this blow." Miss Cantor sniffed, dabbing bloodshot eyes behind metal-rimmed, old-lady glasses. She didn't look mad at us; she looked sad. Sad was better than mad, and it was a good sign that BJ wasn't there. I hoped I wouldn't look like Miss Cantor when I got old: root-bound in this too-small windowless office, like Grandmother Nella's philodendron plant stuck in its old clay pot.

She took a slow breath, let it out in a sigh. "I'm afraid I have some horrible news for you." The smell of her perfume made me queasy. She cleared her throat, fumbled inside her dress to raise a bra strap, adjusted her glasses.

I stole a peek at Midge on my right. She rolled her eyes, looking as confused as I was.

Miss Cantor looked straight at me then, her expression tragic. "It's BJ." Her voice was hesitant. An overhead fluorescent light flickered. "BJ is no longer with us." She reached for her handkerchief. "She passed away late yesterday afternoon—" Miss Cantor interrupted herself with a strangled sob. "Girls, our own Bobby Jo has died."

My eyes wouldn't blink or my brain comprehend. BJ dead? Nobody eighteen years old died. Old people died. Grandmother Nella and Mr. Gordesky, the pharmacist. Not

BJ. She met us every morning by the drinking fountain in front of the school. This was a mistake. A prank. I looked at Miss Cantor for reassurance.

No joke, her eyes said. They were sunk back into her head like she'd gone feeble on us after all these years. Something in my chest constricted. I couldn't catch my breath. BJ was alive Friday night. I'd seen her, a perfectly healthy—though very stuck-up—homecoming queen. And she was okay yesterday, too, because I'd called and talked to her mom.

The room went crooked, the wall clock spinning up toward the ceiling, the wood grain on the massive desk swimming away from me. Miss Cantor's inner-tube middle appeared, pressed against my forehead, steadying the room. "Put your head between your knees, Nella." Her smell was too sweet, her doughy arms too heavy on my shoulders. "Nella, Nella . . . are you all right, dear?"

I fell forward against her into a haze of black nausea, my head swirling as she stroked my hair. When I finally did catch my breath, an unfamiliar weight seemed lodged in my chest. Surely if I cried, it would ease. I tried but couldn't cry. Only more darkness, flickering lights, and faraway sobs from Midge. I swallowed the sounds of my own breath.

"Could you tell us how she died?" Midge's teary voice asked the question.

Miss Cantor stopped rocking me to answer. "She was stung by a wasp at the ranch. A nest that had survived the snowstorms, because it was in their heated barn. She had a massive allergic reaction and was gone before Doc Justice could get there. Anaphylactic shock, they called it. One of those random tragedies that are so shocking." She began

13

rocking me again, the slippery fabric of her skirt chafing now as it rubbed my forehead.

I tried to imagine BJ dead, but her pale-blue eyes smiled back alive from the wildflower meadow at the base of Mount Quandary. The day we'd braided our hair together—my red and her brown—like a lanyard. "Listen to them," she'd whispered, pointing to two baby elk tottering out to the meadow where we lay in tall, wavy grass. "Baby elk have a way they can talk to each other."

BJ dead? I pictured her stretched out on the red velvet lining of a shiny white casket like Grandmother Nella's. But in my imagination, she sat up and frowned at me for that. Busy, bossy, independent, beautiful, mischievous, free. BJ was too alive to be dead. A wasp? I knew her dad was allergic to bee stings, but no one had ever said she was.

Miss Cantor steadied me when I finally sat shakily up-right. Then she walked back behind her own desk and slid a box of Kleenex across to Midge. Her old-lady voice became businesslike. "I have called your mother, Nella, to pick the two of you up." She pulled a pad of pink excuse slips from the drawer BJ had swiped an identical pad our junior year. "I asked that she take you home for the day. I don't want you driving under the circumstances, and I can't imagine you'd get anything out of school today." She opened her black fountain pen and began writing on the top sheet of the pad. "Mr. Gagney has agreed to excused absences. Tomorrow"—she tore off the little pink sheet and handed it across the desk to me, then started writing a second one for Midge—"I'm afraid you'll have a hard job to do. We'll be counting on you senior women to set the example and carry on, help Juniper High return to normalcy."

I fingered my pink slip. Nella Fortune, it said at the top. Excused all day October 28. Reason for excuse—death of friend.

"The funeral, Miss Cantor. When will the funeral be?" Midge, asking the practical questions.

"It was held this morning, dear—a private service. BJ was cremated." Miss Cantor didn't like telling us that; I knew from the tone of her voice. "The Bonnifaces couldn't bear to see any of you. Too grief-stricken." She lowered her eyes..

"Cremated! You've got to be kidding." I said it too loud. "The Bonnifaces would never have a funeral without us. And they wouldn't let anyone burn BJ up, either; I'm sure about that."

Mr. Gagney, the principal, opened the adjoining door from his office, looked at Miss Cantor questioningly, his woolly-worm mustache puckered below his nose. "Smelling salts? Do you need smelling salts?" She shook her head no, waved him away. He looked relieved, quickly closed the door, then reopened it. "Miss Cantor, might I have a word with you when it's convenient?"

"I think they're all right to be left a moment—aren't you, girls?" She stood, followed him into his office, and closed the door.

Midge squatted in front of me the minute the door clicked closed. "Listen to this," she whispered. "Something is bad wrong."

"Of course it is." I sniffed. "BJ's dead. What could be more bad wrong than that?"

"No, it's more than that." Midge's thin, dark eyebrows forked together. "I believe she's dead, and that's awful

15

enough." Her voice lowered. "But I don't think it happened the way Miss Cantor said." She paused to blow her nose on a tissue. "For a change, Nella, you were right and I was wrong." Her eyes, puffy and red-rimmed, locked into mine. "You kept saying it, that BJ just hasn't been herself. And I didn't listen to you." She took both my hands in hers, squeezing them tight as she spoke. "Think about this: something was so wrong that the Bonnifaces couldn't face us. What could have been so bad that they didn't even have a proper funeral?"

chapter three

M om opened her arms when she walked into Miss Cantor's office a few minutes later, and I fell into them. Her familiar softness, the smell of her Wind Song, made things seem sane and solid again. "It's okay, Nella. It's okay, honey."

Mom, making things better. Except this time, she couldn't. Maybe if I hadn't been so blind-jealous when BJ got elected homecoming queen. Maybe if I'd been honest with BJ about what had happened between Rob and me our freshman year. Maybe—just maybe—if I hadn't been so wrapped up in me, I'd have seen Midge's "something is bad wrong."

Mr. Gagney's door opened, and he rushed into Miss Cantor's office, black suit smartly pressed, Rotary Club lapel pin neatly centered. "What a tragedy." He spoke in his syrupy, talking-to-parents voice. "A tragedy! Not once in thirty-one years have I lost a student to a wasp sting. We are most appreciative you could come so expeditiously, Mrs. Fortune." He looked approvingly at my mother in her crisp shirtwaist dress, her dark hair bobbed to the top of her collar. "These girls are in great need of a mother."

The tiny office had become suddenly too hot and small. I was drenched with perspiration. I had to get out.

But getting out and into our familiar silver Buick didn't help much. The car seemed heavy and sad, too, a light rain drizzling over its windshield as Mom drove out of the high school parking lot, past my empty Jeep and the curbside drinking fountain where BJ had waited for us. Mount Quandary was completely hidden under clouds now. Midge, beside me on the front seat, stared at the radio but didn't cut it on. She turned to Mom. "Did you hear about the funeral, Mrs. Fortune?"

Mom nodded yes distractedly with a strange, sad half smile. "Mr. Gagney told me when he called to ask me to come get you."

"How could they have a funeral without us?" Midge twisted red-stained fingers in her lap.

Mom didn't answer, just drove on, staring at the road ahead, her brown eyes misty.

"Honestly, Mom, don't you think it's strange to leave us out of it?" My throat felt tight, my chest heavy with the weight of a hurt I couldn't cry out.

Mom eased the car to a stop at the light. She was wearing those little silver cowboy-hat earrings BJ liked so much. After Mom started down the road again, she talked, and that helped—the familiar voice that miraculously cured church-camp homesickness on a crackling phone line in the three-minute talking limit.

"I don't understand it, either, girls." She shook her head. "Maybe the grief was too bad and they didn't want to prolong it, or"—she shrugged her shoulders like she didn't like saying it—"maybe Em's drinking's gotten so out of hand that Don didn't want to put her through a funeral." Nobody had ever said it out loud before, about BJ's mom and the drinking.

We were behind a run-down pickup with a pale-blue-eyed Australian stock dog in the back. It was sopping wet but wagging its tail happily. I resented it for just being so alive and not understanding that everything was different now.

"I had a cousin once," Midge said over the click, click, click of the windshield wipers. "Buddy. He got dragged to death at Frontier Days. And he was a good saddle bronc rider, too, but his boot got stuck in the stirrup." Her voice lowered to a whisper. "By the time they got the horse stopped, you couldn't even recognize his face." Click, click, click. "This is worse than the day Buddy died."

I could see Midge's point, in a way. Awful things happened to other people's families, but not to people as rich and respected as the Bonnifaces.

+ + +

"You know what we need, Nella?" Mom turned off the ignition. I'd been relieved when we'd dropped Midge off twenty minutes before and was glad to be home in front of the long gray ranch-style house I'd lived in all my life. Inky, my old Labrador retriever, got up slowly and walked across the yard toward us. Three pairs of blue jeans hung stiff-legged on the clothesline in their metal stretchers. Bodies got stiff like that when people died. Rigor mortis.

Mom looked worried when she opened the car door. "Let's go in and make a big bowl of milk toast. I always feel better after milk toast. And some hot tea, too. Hurry, so you don't get wet."

19

It wasn't till I sat across the kitchen table from her, buttery chunks of toast floating in the warm milk in my bowl, that I noticed her eyes were red, too. "Mom," I said, patting Inky's bristly head under the table, "do you really think BJ died from a sting?"

She didn't meet my gaze.

"Midge thinks something's been wrong with BJ for a while—you know, her not calling and everything. Even Mr. Gagney said he'd never had a student die that way."

"I don't know, honey." She poured tea from the old silver pot into two cups, catching the loose leaves in Grandmother Nella's silver strainer. "They say allergies like that run in families, but . . ." She handed me my cup and saucer, took a sip of her tea, and then set it down on the ironed red-checked tablecloth. "It's hard for me to believe, too." She put her fingers together like she was about to say something important, then released them, her voice going practical. "There's not much we can do but face it, Nella. Let's try and freeze what's best about BJ in our memories while we still can." A smile line crinkled the corners of her eyes. "I'll never forget the first time you two met. Do you remember the Thomas Dewey Parade?"

I smiled in spite of myself. "Of course I do. Only they didn't call her BJ then, or even Bobby Jo." I took a spoonful of milk toast; the soggy bread was sweet and soothing. I felt better, snuggled in our cozy, knotty-pine kitchen, talking to Mom, with Inky's warm back pressed against my knee. "She was Roberta Jo. How old were we, about six?"

Mom nodded and dipped her spoon into her bowl. "That would have been 1948. You looked so adorable that day, Nella—those big red bows on your braids. Remember, they put a picture of you and BJ standing by the war memorial on the front page of the *Juniper Press*? You were already a head taller. 'Mutt and Jeff,' your father said."

The Australian stock dog in the pickup flashed back to me. Its eyes were the same pale-blue color as BJ's. Until that day in 1948, I'd never seen a person with eyes that color.

"I didn't like her at first, remember?"

Mom laughed, cornering a piece of bread against the side of the bowl. "Do I ever! Well, she was a curious, ugly duckling child, wasn't she? And you weren't going to let her boss you around."

I shifted my weight, tucked a foot under Inky. Mom was right. We had been equals then. I was every bit as sure of myself as BJ. The difference was that BJ had stayed that way, while it seemed like a little more confidence trickled out of me every year. Maybe it had something to do with how independent she'd become doing her part at the ranch.

Mom's voice brought me back to the kitchen. "Tell me what you remember."

"That's easy." I even recalled what was going on at school that week before I met BJ. For over a month, our first-grade class had followed New York's governor, Thomas E. Dewey, in the fourth grader's leftover *Weekly Readers*. Everyone was sure he'd easily beat Harry Truman and become the next US president. When he announced he'd stop over in Juniper on his way to Cheyenne—something about getting to know people in the heartland—no one believed it at first. Then the town buzzed in preparation. All the storefronts on Main Street were draped in red, white, and blue bunting. One huge banner hung between two cottonwood trees over the street: Juniper, Wyoming, the Littlest Town with the Biggest Heart, Welcomes Thomas E. Dewey.

Midge and I were finally declared old enough to march in a parade. Although I'd never been in one, parades were an important feature in the life of Juniper, so I immediately pictured myself high-stepping along like a Juniper High majorette.

The Saturday of the parade dawned windy and freezing cold. Mom put a pair of her wool socks over my orthopedic Oxfords before I slid them inside galoshes, and she wrapped a hand-knitted red scarf around the collar of my blue snowsuit. "Don't you look patriotic! We're putting on your costume at ten o'clock in front of the Mint Bar. There's a little girl coming in from Big Horn to march with you. Her father's a big Republican donor, too. Try and get to know her, Nella. She doesn't have sisters or brothers, either. She lives on a ranch and doesn't often get to play with other children."

Inky sighed a deep, mournful sigh down there on my foot. "I hated having those mittens pinned to my sleeves, Mom. Do you know I tried to unpin them all day?"

"I'm not surprised." She smiled. "You worked overtime at being grown-up." She reached down and rubbed the calloused skin on Inky's elbow.

"And I hated my costume." Somehow, I'd pictured a hula skirt as something more than red, white, and blue crepe paper strips stapled to a crepe paper band around the outside of my snowsuit. "Except for the Uncle Sam hat and the flag. They at least felt authentic."

We'd waited in front of the Mint Bar for Mr. Bonniface and Roberta Jo, my skirt streamers flapping in the breeze, the sharp winter air going sweetly sour each time someone opened the door of the bar behind us. Up the street in front of the Ben Franklin dime store, a band played "America the Beautiful" as Mom filled me in on the Bonnifaces.

Mr. Bonniface was one of a few really rich ranchers around Juniper. His grandfather had come to Wyoming before the railroad and bought up thousands of acres of land, so they owned one of the biggest Hereford cattle spreads in the state. He, his wife, Emily, and this little girl I had to be nice to lived out on Quandary Creek in a big old ranch house that his grandfather had built.

"Look." Mom had pointed at a shiny black pickup parking across the street. "Here they come now."

A huge man, tall as a totem pole and wearing a red-and-black-plaid hunting jacket, unfolded from the cab of the pickup. He had a strong, masculine face and curly black hair. I watched him lift the little girl down from the pickup's front seat. She was skinny and short, lots shorter than any first grader I knew. Her hair, the color of brown clay, jutted out from each side of her head in two bunches, and she had on big glasses that made her look like the praying mantis in our school terrarium. Roberta Jo was also frowning—a frown so big I could see it from clear across the street.

"Do you remember what happened with BJ's costume?"

Mom nodded. "She never did put on her skirt, did she? And I don't think she marched with you and Midge, either."

"Right and right," I said, remembering. She had on a pink zip-up-the-front snowsuit; nothing red, white, or blue; and was staring right through me with those pale-blue eyes like she had X-ray vision. Creepy. On her feet, though,

23

was a really neat pair of scuffed-up leather cowboy boots. I coveted those.

"I'm not wearing that dumb costume," she told her dad when he tried to staple on her hula skirt. He just nodded, didn't make her put it on or get mad like my dad would if I had done something stupid like not wear my hula costume in a parade. Mr. Bonniface just knelt down and talked to her. I saw then that his eyes were like hers.

About then, Midge came tearing around the corner, the wind whipping her skirt streamers, her dark eyes sparkling under her hat brim. Before I could say a word, she grabbed my hand and began pulling me to the hula welcomers' lineup place. "For crying out loud, Nella, hurry!" she yelled. "We want to be first in the line." So I left Roberta Jo moping and ran to the side street, where we girls locked our arms together in a line right behind the Kaliph Shrine Oriental Band.

When the float up in front of the band started to move, the heavy fake grass on its sides *whushing* along the pavement, I did look for Roberta Jo. She and her father were standing alone behind Boy Scout Troop 10. I waved to her to come with us, but Midge tugging on my arm kept me moving. "Hurry up or we'll lose our place." When we rounded the corner onto Main Street, Roberta Jo was still back there alone, the only Welcoming Girl without a skirt or hat—plus, she had her flag hanging upside down in violation of all the "Let's Honor Our Flag" rules I had been taught.

Midge and I joined right in with the band, singing all the America songs we'd learned at school: "My Country 'Tis of Thee," "God Bless America," "You're a Grand Old Flag." I waved at everyone and forgot all about Roberta Jo till after the parade. Mom had said to wait in front of the war memorial on Courthouse Hill, so I headed there and found Roberta Jo. It was getting cold and had begun snowing hard, little stinging pellets. I balanced my flag on a granite step of the monument so it would stay perpendicular, pulled my snowsuit sleeves down over my mittens, and scrunched my neck down into my coat.

"Aren't you glad to be in a parade now?" I asked Roberta Jo. "Wasn't it just the most fun you've ever had?"

"No," she said, "and I never saw Thomas E. Dewey, either." Maybe she had a cold. Her voice was lower than other girls I knew. I couldn't figure out what to say to a person who didn't like parades.

"Hey," she said, "you got your mittens pinned to your sleeves."

Oh, brother. Talk about embarrassed. "It's just my mom," I said. "She keeps me from losing them this way. You know, like the three little kittens."

"Mama pinned mine on today, too." Roberta Jo smiled, and her slanty eyes behind her glasses squeezed shut. "But I said, 'Take them off or I won't go to the parade.'" Her face looked like the proud leprechaun in *The Blue Fairy Book.* She'd already lost both her front teeth, and I hadn't lost any.

Inky moved away from my leg just then, bringing me back to the kitchen, where Mom sat quietly, watching me. "By the end of that day, she fascinated me, Mom. I'd never known a girl who bossed her own mother around."

Mom shook her head. "Well, BJ had a different kind of family life than most. Her daddy pretty well took her over. Too bad, too, because her mother had a lot to offer a child."

I slipped the towel off the teapot and poured myself more, something inside me craving warmth. "BJ just got away with doing what she wanted to, didn't she?"

Mom's mouth curved into another sad, half-ironic smile. She looked over my shoulder out the kitchen window. "Well, yes and no. I have no way of knowing what actually happened to her." She fingered her teacup, her eyes round and sad in her pretty face. "But I know enough about BJ to wonder whether whatever happened to her yesterday might be one time she didn't get away with it."

chapter four

Dad came home from work that night with worried eyes. "Glad to see you're handling this so well." He patted me on the back. Then to Mom: "We sold two fully loaded sedans today. That makes the month."

Rusty had called three times after school, but Mom took the calls. He just didn't seem that important anymore. "I don't care for any dinner," I said when she set the platter of creamed pork chops on the table. "The milk toast was enough. Think I'll head back to my room."

Dad, looking concerned, turned to Mom, but he seemed reassured when she said I'd already had something to eat. Truth was, even the smell of those pork chops upset my stomach. Plus, I dreaded talking to Dad over dinner. I pretty much knew what he would say to me: "Carry on, Nella. When the going gets tough, the tough get going. You're strong enough to handle this." What I didn't know—really didn't know—was what I would say to him, because I didn't feel tough enough at all.

When I climbed up into my old four-poster bed, the sheets cold and stiff as I slid uneasily between them, it was still hard for me to breathe. I couldn't shake the feeling that I should be able to make sense of it all. What could be so bad? I shivered, pulled the down comforter up to my neck.

Maybe she hadn't gotten away with it this time. How much did Mom know about BJ? There was a whole lot I hoped she didn't. Like last month, on Midge's eighteenth birthday—the first time Mom and Dad had let me have a slumber party in our guesthouse. It was a big party.

All thirteen of us seventeen- or eighteen-year-old girls had sleeping bags on the floor out there in the guesthouse, which stood separate from the main house on the far side of a sweeping lawn Dad took great pride in maintaining himself. Midge had promised us a big surprise that night, and I, at least, was surprised.

When Mom finally left for good with the last of the empty ice-cream bowls, Midge climbed up and stood bare-footed on the couch. Like a revival preacher, she opened a Bible she'd brought with her and crooned, "Ladies, may I introduce you to a little-known text from the time of King David." She began to read from the Song of Solomon, about how King Solomon commands this girl to open her love undefiled to him. He tells her she is tall and slim like a palm tree, and he will climb up into her and take her grape-cluster breasts into his mouth. In the Bible! How did I miss that in three summers at church camp?

"There." Midge slammed the Bible shut and gave BJ, on the floor next to me, a triumphant smile. "I told you it was as good as *Peyton Place.*"

BJ was wearing new pink-and-white-flowered shorty pajamas. No longer the scrawny little praying mantis girl, she'd developed into someone guys couldn't get enough of. When she'd gotten that pixie haircut the end of our soph-omore year plus contact lenses, it had really made her blue eyes pop. She now looked like she could model for *Sixteen* magazine. Her huge boobs—a matter of considerable interest to at least half the boys in the school, from what I could tell—were hard to miss that night under the flimsy material of her pajama top. Barely five feet tall, BJ was definitely King Solomon material, grape clusters and all. "Well," she told Midge, "Song of Solomon is pretty good, but I still like *Peyton Place* better."

"BJ, how did you get your hands on *Peyton Place*?" My voice squeaked when I asked.

BJ wrinkled her nose at me. "I sort of borrow Mom's book from time to time," she said, "from her bedside table, when it doesn't inconvenience her." Everyone in the room laughed. She gave me a worldly smile. "Next time you're at the ranch, remind me, Nella. I'll sneak it out for you. I have a list of the best pages."

"Anyway"—Midge was off on another tangent—"Lexie has borrowed a pack of her dad's Chesterfields for us. Tonight, we will all learn how to look sexy when we inhale. I've watched *Rebel Without a Cause* four times, and I have it down exactly how Natalie Wood does it. If you deliberately drag it out, it drives guys wild." Lexie handed Midge a cigarette package, and Midge curled her shoulder suggestively as she pulled the cellophane band off the top. "So round, so firm, so fully packed. Chesterfields are Mike's very favorite." Another significant look thrown BJ's way.

Teach us to inhale? I didn't even know how to smoke. "Sure," I heard my voice say. "I'm game. Light me up one." And even as I said it, I started worrying about how I'd get the smell of the smoke out of the guesthouse so my folks wouldn't know.

Getting deathly sick smoking that night wasn't even the worst of it. A cold draft woke me at about four thirty, that awful, bitter-stale taste of cigarettes still thick on my tongue. Probably the back door—which I'd deliberately left open till bedtime to clear out the smells—had blown open again. I got up, avoided bodies in sleeping bags strewn across the bedroom floor, and tiptoed in the dark to the tiny kitchen. When my bare feet hit the cold linoleum, I saw that I was right.

Sure enough, the back door was open, moonlight beaming through it.

I gave the door a push to close it, but it didn't budge. I tried again. No luck. Finally, I bent down to check. There was a matchbook wedged under its bottom. Somebody must have sneaked out. Dad would kill me if he found out!

When I stepped outside onto the smooth flagstone patio, a huge moon was spotlighting the yard, and a dog barked. I waited a minute, wondering where to look and for whom, when I heard a car motor running at the far end of our long circular driveway. The drive was rimmed with a shoulder-high hedge, so I bent low in its shadow and walked toward the sound till I saw Calvin's black-and-white car parked at the far end of our drive. A sickening feeling came over me as I peeked through the hedge, my own memories of Rob in that car rushing back.

Brother, of all the cars I did not want parked there, Calvin Sharpe's would head the list. It wasn't just the car; Calvin himself unnerved me in a titillating, scary way. He wore his black hair slicked back in a ducktail, and he moved like a panther. My mouth went dry every time he looked at me, though he hardly ever said anything. He was sexy in the way James Dean was, and unquestionably the wildest guy in the senior class.

"We're getting low on petrol." Calvin's snarly voice. He leaned forward in the driver's seat and turned off the ignition, then twisted toward the back seat, which was blocked from my view by the thick hedge. "Well, shit, Rob. No wonder we're cold up here. You two polar bears back there just might have to roll up the window."

My stomach knotted. BJ must be in the back seat with Rob. I moved to a thinner part of the hedge, bending forward to get a better look, scratching my cheek as I did. A shaft of moonlight lit up the back of Rob's curly dark head.

My breasts tingled, remembering Rob's touch, his electricity felt in my body, the sweetness of his tongue in my mouth. King Solomon echoed in my ears. *I will climb into your tree and eat your fruit.* I knew I should leave but couldn't make myself do it. I felt embarrassed, jealous, shocked, and—in spite of myself—intensely curious. Like watching *Peyton Place* in real life.

A familiar laugh from the front seat. Lexie Medina. Well, that wasn't surprising. I'd heard she was that kind of girl, but BJ? Maybe they'd been drinking. Mom said boys tried to get girls to drink so they'd lose their inhibitions.

Rob's face disappeared in the shadow of the hedge, then reappeared—then disappeared. Someone moaned; it sounded like BJ. Were they having sex right there in the back seat of Calvin's car? Were Lexie and Calvin doing the same thing up front?

My ankles wobbled, sour water rising in the back of my throat. I couldn't watch any longer. The dog barked again. I froze, afraid it might draw their attention to me. But all

I heard was another moan from the back seat, so I crept back along the hedge and back to the guesthouse. I left the matchbook in place, felt my way to my sleeping bag, and climbed in, glad for its fuzzy warmth on my frozen feet. At least one thing I didn't have to worry about was the smoke smell, with the door open all night long.

I lay awake in sick confusion for a real long time. Those same hands—Rob's hands—had crept under my blouse and into my bra. And I'd just let him do it, even though I was betraying BJ. Might even let it happen again if I had the chance. Other guys didn't affect me the way Rob did. If Sheriff Madsen hadn't shown up that night, the big spotlight on his truck searching the Wyoming Girls' Reform School fields for poachers, I'm not sure we'd have stopped. What right did I have to judge BJ? But there was something so public, so tasteless, about making out when two other people were in the car. Had BJ and I grown that different from each other?

Finally, I did sleep, and in muddled dreams, it was my breasts Rob stroked in the back seat of Calvin's car. I didn't hear anyone come back in, but BJ and Lexie were there in the morning, acting perfectly normal. Nobody asked me about the scratch on my face, and I never told anyone what I'd seen. Actually, I tried to forget it.

I hoped BJ would bring it up one day and we'd talk. She'd say, "Boy, I really messed up, sneaking out the night of your slumber party—and drinking, too. I got off lucky." We'd laugh about it together, be glad it happened only that once, and maybe I'd even tell her the truth about Rob and me.

But now, of course, that day could never come.

chapter five

I n my bed, I couldn't stop running the film strip of my BJ memories. I plumped my pillow, turned off the lamp, and closed my eyes. Little bits of light flickered with her face floating between them: "I've something in my pocket . . . It's a great big Brownie smile." Pony rides through the woods at full gallop. Buck, their foreman, pulling me out of a foot of muddy water when Domino jumped an irrigation ditch and I fell off. The strange vibrations between BJ's parents, half-magnetic, half-angry. Maria, their cook, more like a mother to BJ than her own—it seemed to me—doing her best to do right by her.

We'd eaten early at the long dining room table one summer night—just Mrs. Bonniface, BJ, and me—with the usual white linens and lighted silver candlesticks. After dinner, her mom excused herself for the kitchen, then reappeared. She passed us at the table without speaking, the ice in her drink glass tinkling as she walked down the back hall to her bedroom.

As soon as her mom had left, BJ motioned for me to follow her into the kitchen. Maria was at the sink, doing the dishes. "We're going to see Standing Elk," BJ told her. "We'll be back before dark."

Standing Elk, this ancient Indian man who lived several miles away from the big house out at the Bar Z, was BJ's favorite person. He had skinny gray braids that snaked down the middle of his back, and eyes that sank like a mystery deep into his skull. I loved his voice, a voice so quiet you had to listen hard to hear his secrets: how to make whistles out of willows, how to tell someone was coming by putting your ear to the ground, where the paintbrush bloomed first in the spring, which leafy green plant cured rope burns, even how to find tiny mouse skeletons in the turds of an owl.

There was a predictability about Standing Elk. Nothing ever made him too happy or too sad. He usually sat in his only chair—a bent metal one with a torn red oilcloth seat— while we squatted on the ground by his campfire, straining red dirt as fine as women's face powder, through our fingers. At sunset, we'd watch the sun paint brilliant colors on the sky above Mount Quandary. Standing Elk's camp was the perfect vantage point. Smells of sage and clean grass hung in the air. We'd listen for the yip of a coyote, the rustle of a nighthawk, the whisper of the cottonwood trees. "It is the way," Standing Elk told us, "Great Spirit talks to you." I felt safer there by Standing Elk's campfire than anywhere else on the Bar Z.

That night, though, Maria frowned as she picked up a dish towel and pointed at the clock. "Too late," she said crossly in her heavy Mexican voice. "You don't have no time, lest you cross the river and the stud pasture, and you know better." She skimmed soapy lather off her wide brown arm.

"We'll just go to the barn, then." BJ ducked under Maria's arm, motioning for me to follow her as she ran out the back door.

"BJ," Maria called after us, "you stay out of that stud pasture." Her voice got louder. "Your papa, he'll have my hide, he catches you in there again. You'll get yourself bad hurt."

"Come on, Nella." BJ was halfway across the yard and waving impatiently at me. "Hurry up."

When I caught up, she said, "Don't pay any attention to Maria. We'll turn back the other way when she can't see us."

When we were in the trees and out of sight of the house, BJ changed direction, heading back toward the big log that lay across the river. She was taking the exact shortcut Maria had warned her not to take. I really didn't want to follow her, but I did.

The log we had to cross was at least ten feet long across the widest and deepest part of Quandary Creek. BJ went first, talking the whole way. When it was my turn, I held my breath and forced myself not to look down into the swift-flowing current below. Looking down was what made you dizzy, BJ said.

I took a relieved breath when I'd made it and swatted at a mosquito that had buzzed me all the way across. Then I saw the stallion. "Oh no, BJ!" I yelled at her. "Canadian's in the stud pasture. We can't go this way." He was on the far side, the biggest horse I'd ever seen—thick-necked and massive, like Grandmother Nella's grand piano. About the same dark color, too. So big he'd squish you if he stepped on you. I liked feeding him sugar cubes when he was in his stall at the barn with a gate between us. His muzzle was soft like moss on stream rocks, and his tongue tickled as it twisted across my palm, looking for sugar. "Hold your hand real flat," BJ had warned me. "You don't, and he'll chew your finger up with the sugar."

BJ ignored my warnings that night, just like she had Maria's. She climbed between the middle and bottom strands of the barbed wire fence right into the stud pasture. "He's not going to hurt us!" she yelled when she got inside. "C'mon, Nella."

My heart pounded in my ears as I slipped through the barbed wire into the pasture. She put both fingers to her mouth and whistled for Canadian, the shrill kind of whistle that movie cowboys make. On the far side, he raised his head, whinnied, and began trotting toward us.

"Maria doesn't know what she's talking about." BJ whistled again and skipped toward him, her skinny brown ponytail bouncing up and down as Canadian galloped toward her. I stayed near the fence. His hooves made loud thudding sounds, throwing big clods of black dirt out behind him. "C'mon, Nella, he'd never hurt a flea." She was headed right for him, this little insect-size girl, her right hand going to her jean-jacket pocket where she kept the sugar cubes.

I took about two steps in their general direction, then stopped again—the horse was way too close for comfort. I half squinched my eyes closed so I wouldn't see him run her over, my heart tightening in my chest, my eyes wanting to shut completely. At the last-possible minute, though, he skidded to a stop, dust and dirt flying in all directions. Then he reached out his huge head to her open hand and made a beautiful chuckle sound in the back of his throat.

When the dust had settled, BJ yelled back at me over her shoulder, impatient this time. "C'mon, Nella! What you waiting for, Christmas?"

From where I was standing, I could hear him crunch the sugar cubes in those giant teeth. He nuzzled her shoulder for more. I quietly began walking toward him. As I got closer, I could smell his wonderful mixture of horse and alfalfa and leather.

Thank heavens, he paid no attention to me, just kept butting BJ with his head. She giggled, held him by his halter till he raised his head and lifted her several inches off the ground, then back down. She gave him another sugar cube to thank him for the ride. I kept her between Canadian and me since I didn't have any treats and I wasn't wanting a ride.

Finally, she turned her back on him and skipped to the far side of the fence. He followed like a puppy, so I ran in a wide circle to get ahead of her. I could hear the heaving of his breath behind us. When we'd climbed back through the barbed wire to the far side—me first—he nickered softly, like he was laughing at me for being afraid.

"He doesn't want us to leave," she said. "Poor baby; he's trying to talk us into coming back."

So she'd been right again. It was what amazed me most about BJ—how she knew when to listen to grown-ups and when not to.

She had run on ahead of me that night toward Standing Elk's shack, then stopped to look up the channeled trunk of the big cottonwood tree there. "Darn," she said when I caught up. "He's not here."

"How can you tell?"

"No birds—his ravens."

I looked up. Cottonwood fluff hung thick in the air, but the three black birds that stayed close to Standing Elk were missing.

"He's probably fishing or something. Some nights, he walks clear to the top of Mount Quandary and stays without even a bedroll. Doesn't eat, either. Fasting, he calls it." A devilish smile crossed her face. "Let's go back the long way by the bridge and see if he's fishing there. We'll miss the stud pasture." The way BJ smiled, I knew she understood I was relieved.

Just before the bridge, when the light in the painted sky had faded to a dull blue gray, we spooked a nighthawk, and I jumped a country mile. BJ took my hand and held it tight. The mountains were throwing pointed shadows across their yard when we walked down the driveway toward the house, still holding hands.

chapter six

Finally—hours later, it seemed—I was falling asleep, mercifully asleep, but Midge's question jolted me back awake. What could have been so bad? My head pounded, my breath grew short. I wasn't going to rest until I made sense of it.

I sat up and reached for the lamp on my bedside table. The soft-yellow light chased away some of the goblins. *Magnificent Obsession*, in its well-worn blue cover, sat stacked on two scrapbooks there. I propped pillows behind me, pushed my hair out of my face, reached for the top scrapbook, and started flipping pages. BJ and I'd stuck the little picture-holding corners on page one at least ten years ago. Some of them were peeling away from the page.

One day last summer, we'd pulled the scrapbook out and laughed over the pictures: "Can you believe how frizzy those perms were?"

"Your fringed cowgirl skirt was my favorite."

"I wanted your boots."

"Look, we're getting boobs—well, you are, BJ."

"Remember how you stole Marvin from me at camp?"

"You can have him back." Always with BJ, the wonderful, husky little-girl laugh. I felt newly alone in the puddle of lamplight, a world of darkness surrounding my bed now that BJ was no longer in it.

I flipped more pages. Lots of birthday-party pictures. She gave me my favorite presents because she knew me best: nylon—we called them silk—panties embroidered with the days of the week, whose dictates we carefully observed when we dressed ourselves. Delicious gardenia-scented Friendship Garden bubble bath in pastel paper packets. Tubes of plastic bubble-blowing stuff with little straws attached. And the Magic 8 fortune-teller ball that invariably answered our most pressing questions with the floating words *Signs point to yes*.

There we were on Palm Sunday in the Saint Peter's Episcopal Church Junior Choir, proud and pious in our white cottas and black skullcaps, small palm crosses pinned on our shoulders. My face was covered with freckles, my hair was in French braids, and I was a full head taller than BJ. Both my front teeth were missing; hers had already come in over-big and gopherish. We sang a duet together: "Were You There When They Crucified My Lord?" I'd asked BJ what it meant to tremble: *Sometimes, it causes me to tremble.*

"You shake all over," she said, "from the inside out."

Another picture in the church. This time it's Easter. We're wearing hand-smocked dresses and matching black patent Mary Janes. We went together with our mothers to buy the shoes, the kind of thing real sisters would do. BJ had her feet x-rayed three times in the shoe-fitting machine so she could count her foot bones.

Tears burned my eyes as I set the album on the table, turned out the light, and kept on remembering.

Her white lace bra. She'd bought it herself when we were thirteen. "Mom hasn't noticed I need one," she said, "so I got it yesterday at Stevens Fryberger. You can borrow it fifth period, but Midge has dibs sixth." It was pretty uncomfortable, but I stuffed it with toilet paper and gave it a try. Danny Owensby stared at my chest with keen interest all through social studies but looked puzzled and disappointed in sixth-period math.

The Bar Z—so many memories of the ranch. The sweet, heavy hay smell of the barn when we put our cheeks to the side of their dairy cow, Buttercup, listening to the underwater sloshes and gurgles from her unborn calf, BJ's future 4-H project. The miracle of being there two weeks later when the calf was born, all beautifully new, wide-eyed, and wobbly-legged. We named her Molly and watched her nurse the first time. *Oh, BJ, how can life ever be right without you?*

At least she'd gotten to be homecoming queen the very last weekend of her life. She'd looked so cold and unhappy, sitting there in the convertible before the parade, that I ran to get her a cup of hot coffee. Rob grabbed it before BJ could touch it, spilled it all over her skirt, and then acted like it was my fault, not his. As the convertible pulled away from the curb, I waved at her and smiled. It was a hard thing for me to do. She'd ignored my wave, looked right past me, the blue-and-gold crepe paper banners tied to the antenna snapping in the wind. *A poor winner*, I'd thought.

But there was more to it than that. Her eyes looked preoccupied. Not happy or falsely humble like other homecoming queens. *Preoccupied* really was the right word. Why? She'd hated the Thomas Dewey Parade, so maybe BJ just disliked parades. No, I couldn't imagine anyone hating being a homecoming queen. "Remember, BJ," I'd yelled at her, "smile real big because you never know when you'll get to be in another parade!" Gag! What had made me say that?

I shivered—trembled, really—grateful when the sobs finally rose into my throat. Muffling the sounds in my pillow, I cried for hours—or was it long minutes?—until the memory hit. Lit up in Technicolor, a memory so powerful I sat straight up in bed. Our end-of-the-summer picnic at Tomahawk Lake.

I see it all now, a moment of perfect recall shimmering before me. The six of us are lying near the water on BJ's dad's old navy blankets, soaking up the sun one last time before Mike leaves to go back to Laramie—Mike and Midge, BJ and Rob, Rusty and me. Rob is propped on his right arm and extends his hand. "Hand me that last brew, Mike."

Midge wanders down to the water's edge to throw her sandwich crusts to the ducks. "Wait." Mike jumps up, runs after her. "Don't throw them away. If you don't want them, I do."

Midge smiles and deliberately lobs the crusts to the ducks. "You got a tapeworm or something? Ducks have to eat, too, you know."

BJ, laughing at Midge, sits up to watch and hooks the toes of her left foot over the top of Rob's ankle. Suddenly, her eyes widen in surprise. Her foot jerks away from Rob. She screams and rolls off the blanket. She's standing, jumping up and down, obviously doesn't realize she's turned over the last precious bottle of his beer and it's gurgling into the sand. "Get it off, Rob! Get it off! Geez, it hurts!"

Rob is on his feet, grabbing a towel and popping off a bee that's stuck to BJ's bare skin on her back, right above the silver-blue line of her swimsuit.

Mike rips open a pack of Chesterfields and hands cigarettes to Rob, who tears them open and wets them with the little bit of beer left in the bottle. He holds BJ against him, both arms around her. With his right hand, he presses the tobacco against her back. The sun setting over the rim of the lake lights them in silhouette. The tobacco seems to be helping. She's stopped squirming. Her body's pressed tight against his—a beautiful scene.

She looks up at him gratefully. Her lower lip quivers. "Bees must have it in for me or something. This is my third sting this summer."

chapter seven

JUPITER, WYOMING

Thursday, October 15, 1959

Jesus, BJ had been in Doc's office forever. How long could it take to figure out something like that? I drummed my fingers on the dash of the pickup, wished I was home heating up a little Chef Boyardee before football practice.

From where I'd parked in front of Doc Justice's office, I could barely pick out Mount Quandary's head sticking up between two gray clouds like it was pissed at me, too. Doc's office is the last building on Spruce Street. Then Juniper just ends, and big, wide cow pastures fill in the space out toward the mountains and the Bar Z. The mountains circle Juniper so tight they block out the rest of the world. Only one TV station gets over them. Up in Billings, a hundred and fifty miles north, they have three. Reminds me of that snow fort I built around our house the winter I was ten and Dad still lived with us. Back then, I'd thought nothing too bad could happen in Juniper. That snow forts and mountains would block out the bad shit of the world.

What was keeping BJ so long? Man, my mouth was dry. Worry dried me out that way. I could have used a cherry Coke.

44

I remembered the picture of the sperm and the egg in my biology book, a tadpole boring a hole in a ball. Never could figure out how you got a baby out of that. I shrugged, turned up Elvis on the radio. "Hound Dog."

At least it was raining. Otherwise, I would have been at Juniper High, throwing pass patterns, exactly twenty minutes ago. No way Coach Robbins would call off practice except for rain, with homecoming a week and a day away and the state championship riding on the game.

I stuck my hand in my jeans pocket and rubbed my lucky buckeye. So far, so good. I'd dodged lying to Coach about why I wouldn't be there. I could picture him now, that big cliff over his eyes lowering into a frown, his voice as serious as Sergeant Friday on *Dragnet*. "No girlfriend, Rob—not even Bobbie Jo Bonniface—is worth missing practice. Football is your future, boy! It's your ticket outta this one-horse town."

Well, what was going on with BJ was my future, too, but Coach didn't need to know that. I rubbed my buckeye again. If my luck held, he never would. I'd practice extra hard next week. Coach thought I had a real shot at making the all-star team if we beat Casper. Best high school quarterback in the state of Wyoming. That ought to make the ole man proud . . . wherever he was.

I picked up my social studies book, pulled out a sheet of paper, and tried memorizing the names in the executive branch. At least I knew the first two. President Eisenhower and Vice President Nixon had been doing it so long, everybody knew them. But the cabinet members didn't want to stick. I looked back at the mountains; it was snowing up on Mount Quandary. My brain couldn't think about government shit or chemical elements, especially not those lines from *Romeo and Juliet*. I had to know about BJ first. Then I'd go home and try and try to cram it in my head. Jesus, it seemed like I'd been waiting out here six months.

She hadn't liked that I didn't go in with her. Maybe I shouldn't have let her go in alone. "You're a rat fink," she'd said as she slammed the pickup door. But girl stuff embarrassed me. Probably shouldn't have, since I was living with just Mom and Rose before Rose married Carl, but it always had. They hung their wet underwear and nylon stockings all over the bathroom. Wanted me to buy them feminine hygiene products when I was at the drugstore. Embarrassing. I would just look the other way, try to get out of doing it. Anyhow, BJ had told me it was okay to wait out front. Doc Justice had brought her into the world, she said, took out her tonsils when she was seven, gave her iron when she got low blood from her periods, stuff like that.

I was noticing how rotten everything looks when the snow gets washed away. It was snowing when we'd pulled up at three fifteen—big, wet flakes, the kind you want for hardpack snowballs. But after BJ had left, it turned into sleet, and then a cold misery of a rain pouring down my windshield like I'd parked under a waterfall. Big clods of dirt sticking out of the snow on the street. I didn't mind snow. You can sled on snow. But rain—now, rain's different. It muddies up things, makes dirt goopy like chocolate pudding. You ever try to run laps on a dirt track in rain, you know what suffering is.

I'd heard once they had to do awful things up inside a girl to see if she was going to have a kid. I hoped BJ was all right, tried picturing her. So little and soft, the way her eyes slanted at the corners when she looked up at me. Lightest blue eyes I'd ever seen, with gold flecks in them. The color of that cavalry sword on the wall of the Mint Bar, hard-to-see-through eyes that made me happy when they smiled back. Which they hadn't been doing much of these past few weeks.

She was the one who made the call to Doc Justice when she still hadn't gotten a period this month. BJ didn't bleed like a stuck pig every month the way Rose did; she just got one every couple of months. So at first, there was nothing to worry about. But then, last week, she'd begun worrying and talked to me about it. "Something weird is going on in my belly. There's a hard lump, and I'm getting poochie. Plus, I've never gone four months without a period. Do you think I could have gotten pregnant just that one time we didn't use a rubber?"

Shit, I didn't have any idea about stuff like that. So I just listened to what she thought and was glad we wouldn't tell any parents till she'd gone to see Doc. I decided on that day, though, and told her that I wanted to take her to Doc's even if it meant missing a day of practice. I might have to tell Coach a lie, but this was important. I had to go with her even though I dreaded the hell out of the idea.

My stomach growled. Man, I was starving. I watched the water drip off the end of the wipers, ran my fingers in and out of a tear in the vinyl seat cover to pass the time. What was it BJ had said about my fingers that day last summer out at Tomahawk Lake? That my fingers and my ears—the way my ears stuck close to my head—looked engineered, designed special just for me. "All of you," she said, "is so tight and hard and efficient. And your hands are

47

good for more than just throwing balls." She leaned her head sideways, the way she did when she was joking. I think she was feeling a little shy about what had just happened.

We'd driven out to the lake late that afternoon when I got off work and—like always—laughed at the sign: No lifeguard on duty. Proceed at your own risk. Because it was June, and I'd been working all month, including all that day, at the Juniper Municipal Pool, lifeguarding. We still had our suits on. I spread her dad's old navy blanket out on the sand for us to lie on and flipped the bottle top off my brew, took a long drink, and handed it to her. She wasn't much of a drinker, but she liked the taste of Coors, so I got my buddy, Pork, to buy me Coors when he made beer runs up to Montana.

Looking back at what happened, I'm pretty sure BJ had decided ahead that this was going to be *the* day. Instead of taking a little sip, she drank a great big slug of my beer and kept a hold of the bottle, drinking away till she finished the whole thing. It surprised me, but I didn't say anything, just opened another one up for myself. I'd bought three, was thinking I should have bought more as I lay down next to her.

I began noticing things I never had before: The way the little hairs on her arms sparkled in the sun. The white smallpox circle scar at the top of her arm. Two funny-looking blackbirds with red and yellow on their wings, saying, "Tweedledee," back and forth to each other out by the lake. And these dragonflies stuck together over the marsh, hooked up and hanging like a helicopter over the cattails. Bright blue with see-through light-up wings, like the sun was caught inside them.

She pointed. "Look, Rob. They fly while they're doing it."

"Dragonflies got the right idea." I gave her my teasing smile because I'd been trying to talk her into the same thing for two years. Had even tried to get some Spanish fly from an ole buddy of Dad's when he drove a shipment of sugar beets down to Mexico, but he forgot to look for me.

I was behind her, shoving my finger along the little empty place over her collarbone before I began to work my way down. I leaned forward, like I was trying to get a better look at the dragonflies, began rubbing my right hand over the top of her two-piece suit while I got my left hand on the clasp and slid her top off. Her bare tits went hard under my finger. So far, so good. I raised myself up on an elbow for a better look. I never got tired of looking at BJ's world-class tits. I turned her around, pulled her toward me, and kissed one.

"Maybe," I said as I pinched her nipple and tugged on it, "dragonflies are smarter than you think because they enjoy it while they can." She was swelling, getting hotter. My big hands barely covered her breast now. "You wait till you're married, you could die an old-maid dragonfly." She smiled, French-kissed me back, and pushed her hips against mine.

I was catching fire, so I tried what I had a million times before: putting a hand inside her suit bottom on the soft skin of her ass. This time, she didn't stop me, so I pulled her closer. My blood was starting to boil; this could be it. I made myself take it slow, soft-rubbing her ass—not as big as a football, but a perfect handful—and working my hand down to the smooth skin between her legs, where she was already wet. She twisted into me, rubbing against that hand, circling her tit in my right hand. Jesus, I was melting inside. She had never let me go this far. When it seemed like the right time, I eased myself out of my jock and pulled my swimsuit to one side to free up my dick. BJ felt it happen, looked straight into my eyes, nodded her head, and spread her legs. I knew then it was okay. I kissed her with all the tongue and lips I could find, my whole body saying how much I loved her as I slid in.

No guy in his right mind would have thought about a rubber at a time like that. She just goddamn opened up to me, the smell of her down there like a hot, wet greenhouse. I never even got the bottom of her suit off, just slid inside the stretchy elastic leg of it. Her smell, the way she moved—shit, I didn't last long. I heard her suit leg tear just as I came inside her. Afterward, I made it good for her, too, being as it was her first time. All those girls I'd fucked my first year of high school—for a while, I couldn't fuck enough of them—they had taught me plenty. Then, with my thumb, I ran a pretend zipper up her belly. "I'm closing you up, Beej. You're my woman now. No other guy can lay a hand on you."

She smiled at my zipper finger, followed it with her eyes to the leg of her swimsuit, which was flapping loose, torn clear across, and covered in a little blood. "Well, there," she said. She was still out of breath. "That was better than wonderful. I'm tired of doing everything but the real thing. Two and a half years is long enough to wait. It's hypocritical."

I didn't know for sure what *hypocritical* meant, but I was damn glad she felt that way. She raised up her face to mine, staring hard, the blue color in her eyes going deeper, like something was making her sad. Then she put her head back on my chest. "I'm not the first for you, though, am I?

You really knew what you were doing." Her lips tickled my chest hair as she talked. She rolled away from me, flat on her back, giving me a full side view of those magnificent tits.

"You smell like a greenhouse full of lilacs, BJ. I don't want to talk about the others. They were all before you. They didn't mean a thing to me."

"You knew just what to do with your hands, Rob. It was amazing." She shook her head like I had really surprised her. "You're as good at making love as you are at throwing a football, better than all the descriptions in *Peyton Place*." She stretched, arched her back like a naked cat.

The air was cooling off, the sun going down, making me get goose bumps—or was it what had just happened? I was getting another hard-on just watching her. I took a drink of my brew, adjusted myself so she wouldn't notice that. The sky out past the lake was so pink and orange it colored us, too. I couldn't believe BJ was still lying there half-naked, like somebody with a paint can had come along, dipped in their brush, and painted her with pink cream. The dragonflies showed up again, too, still hitched together. Their wings matched the sky and BJ's pink body. "All the others before, they were just practice for you, Beej."

What I said to her wasn't bullshit, either. I meant every word. She blew me away—that smooth, skinny belly under her huge, round tits; the way her legs bent and stretched like rubber bands; how ready she was for me. She was so quiet, like an orchestra violin playing. And that smell like lilacs, the way springtime smells at my gramma's house. I didn't just climb on BJ and fuck her the way I had all the others. I'd noticed her the second day of high school, our freshman year. Never had seen her before because she'd just come in from a county school. We had started dating right away, but I waited two and a half years—two and a half long years— till she was ready, and God, it was worth the wait.

But now, man, I couldn't believe I was sitting here in the pickup, waiting to see if she was knocked up. What a waste of money. All those rubbers every time since, and she may have gotten pregnant that first day at Tomahawk Lake.

The very next weekend, I'd shown her a rubber and told her we'd have to use it to be safe. I'd learned all about rubbers from Carl, my brother-in-law, who gave me my first pack in a dark corner of our backyard on my fourteenth birthday. The most useful present I ever got.

She touched it with her finger. "I'm glad you know about these things. I've seen them, but I've never actually touched one. It's the color of the pink rubber baby dolls I used to play with in my dollhouse. Maybe there's a connection, eh?"

"Yeah," I said. Wondered what she meant.

She watched me put it on. I could see her nipples getting hard under her shirt. She didn't have any of that fake being-modest stuff like a lot of girls I knew. Sometimes she almost got me embarrassed at myself. But inside, I was pretty proud of how big I got. She smiled, reached out, and touched my dick with the rubber on it. "It feels like rubber. I get it." We both laughed.

I pushed her down on the pickup seat under me, rubbed her to get her ready. Then I opened her up and drove my-self in. My butt knocked the horn once when I pumped up crooked, scared the shit out of us for just a second. But it didn't matter, because no one else was out there on the empty road by the Wyoming Girls' Reform School.

BJ was a real fast learner. Got to the place we couldn't hardly stand it till we got off by ourselves. Even the first time, though, she was the best lay I ever had. I didn't figure anyone would outdo Lexie Medina, who was probably the first lay for half the guys in Park County. That girl couldn't get enough of you. BJ, though, just seemed to know how to move, and I was her first and only one.

Hard to believe that twelve weeks had passed, and BJ still hadn't gotten a period. Man, I saw the baby connection now.

They were playing all Elvis on KWYO. "Jailhouse Rock" didn't help. I cut the radio off, wondered if they could can a guy for knocking up a rich rancher's only daughter. BJ's dad had always treated me like a missing son, but fathers can go crazy when things happen to their daughters. I'd heard stories. I decided to stop worrying till I knew for sure. Maybe something else had been making her puke every morning, some germ that made you miss your period, too.

The tops of the mountains were solid white when she finally came out Doc's door. My gut twisted. I took one look at her and knew we were busted. It looked like Doc had shrunk her when he stuck his tools inside her. She looked sick and small, standing there outside the door with the rain beating down on her blue parka. All I wanted was to wrap myself around her and make it better. I opened the door and sprinted across the parking lot. The mud was thick as axle grease. Seemed like I was running in slow motion, like I'd never get her into my arms. She watched me, tears and rain dripping down her face, her eyes looking so big and helpless.

When I got to her, she fell against me like she needed help standing. BJ, who always knew what to do, didn't say anything, just stuck her face into my shoulder and cried.

"Beej, honey," I said, feeling so shitty and helpless. "We'll think of something. It'll be all right. I promise." I got her in the truck and reached in my pocket for my handkerchief.

"He says I'm almost four months pregnant, Rob." Her voice was high, panicky-sounding. "I will look more than *poochie* this time next month."

I tried to dry her hair with my handkerchief. Her eyelids were blinking back tears, the way windshield wipers push away rain. "Let's go out to the lake. We'll sort it out better there."

"I can't go now," she said in a butterfly whisper. "I've got to get back to school. I'm in charge of the homecoming skit for Pep Club."

"Jesus, can't somebody else run a fucking skit practice?"

"I really have to." Her voice sounded shaky. "But if you'll pick me up at six, I'll call the ranch and tell Maria I have to stay in town for another meeting."

"Okay." I turned the truck back toward Juniper High. "We need some time to talk it out. That's all. I'll wait in front of the gym for you."

She didn't smile at me when she got out. Just walked away like a stranger. The rain had slowed down some. I rolled down my window. "I love you!" I yelled at her back. She nodded, but she didn't turn around.

chapter eight

I drove straight to the edge of town, parked in the Safeway lot, got out, and headed for the hills. I ran till I couldn't run anymore. Then I puked my guts out over the side of a rocky gray cliff. It felt good to puke. It was barely drizzling now. I stayed up there on the hill, feeling as sad as those Stephen Foster songs in grade school, rubbing my buckeye for good luck and help.

I told myself it was like an algebra problem, all those x's and y's not making sense till you knew how to look at them. I tried to think it out till my head began to pound and I couldn't think at all. So I took a break.

Down below me in Juniper, little lights were starting to come on in town. I admired the lights till the pounding let up. Gradually, an idea about what I should do started coming through. It got clearer, then so clear I jumped up like a load had been lifted and headed for Safeway, hoping it would still be open. I wanted to see how many hours I could work and still stay in school. I knew I'd have to stay in school.

Mr. Quackenbush looked surprised when I found him in the produce section. "Rob Hitchcock? Get yourself over here. You must have grown a foot since last spring. What are you, six two? Six three?"

"Yes, sir," I said. "Six three. I've still got the buckeye you gave me, Mr. Quackenbush." I pulled it out of my pocket to show it to him. "I'm glad you're still here. I heard you were going to retire."

"Well, I changed my mind, decided it's better to wear out than rust out." He was rubbing his hands back and forth over a giant purple-and-white turnip like he was polishing a diamond. Mr. Quackenbush really loved his produce. He was a long-headed guy with a bald, high-domed forehead who smiled this big happy smile when he got his hands in the vegetables. "And I missed my produce. Get a gander at the most beautiful turnip I've ever seen! A real champion!" He rubbed the turnip again, this time with the edge of his apron. "Out of California. Boy, do they know how to grow them out there." He stopped smiling all at once when he noticed the look on my face.

I put the buckeye back in my pocket. "I need to talk to you, sir."

He set his turnip on a packing crate, wiped his hands on his white apron. "So, son, what's up?"

For a minute, I was afraid I'd break down and cry, but I got it all spit out. That I was thinking about quitting football before the season was over to come back and work as much as possible. He reached for my shoulder, touched me easy—like I was a prize turnip, too—his eyes looking worried. "You okay, boy?" I'd give my left nut if my own ole man cared half as much about me as Mr. Quackenbush did. He squeezed my shoulder. "I know your old man's boozing, left home again. Anything I can do to help, Rob?"

"Could you give me my job back, sir?" The light flicked in the display case. I looked over at it, stopped the tears before they got to my eyes, but I could tell he'd noticed. "Nothing's wrong, Mr. Quackenbush. I just got a damn good deal on a '57 T-Bird and I want it real bad, so I'm quitting the team." It was hard to lie to Mr. Quackenbush.

He shook his head like he didn't like the idea. "Don't make a grain of sense to me," he said. "Good a quarterback as you are, only a couple of games to go. We're all cheering for you, boy. You have a real chance for a scholarship down at the university."

"I know, Mr. Quackenbush, but I've made up my mind. I'm in good shape. I can load anything. Couldn't you use an extra stock boy right now?"

"Rob, if your old man was here, he'd tell you to give up the car, keep on with the football, and get a college education. But I'm not your old man—and of course I could always use a good worker." His hand slipped off my shoulder. "Tell you what let's do: I'll hold your job. You finish the season—what you got, two, three weeks more?—and I promise you can work overtime to make as much money as you need after that. But don't quit now, Rob. There's too much hanging on the season."

"Yes, sir. Thanks, Mr. Quackenbush. I'll do it that way." I shook his hand. "It's a deal."

I got out of Safeway fast as I could, made a point of not looking at my lying self in the mirror behind the produce. By the time I cranked the truck and headed for Juniper High to go get BJ, I was a married man in my head. Once I got over the shock of the idea, I thought, *Shit, I might even get used to this.* Graduation was sneaking up on us. I didn't like the idea of BJ going off to Massachusetts to some fancy girls' college. I started getting excited, thinking about us together for good.

Before Grandpa had died, he told me about trouble, how it has a way of finding you. "Everyone eats brown bread sometime, Robbie boy." Well, maybe this was just brown-bread time for Beej and me. We'd face up to it the best we could.

As I drove back to Juniper High, I thought about how Rose had looked before she had Carl Jr., and tried picturing BJ pregnant with my little pink kid growing in her belly. Skinny little Beej, hardly five feet tall, with a basketball pushing her belly button inside out, my boy inside her, hammering away with his arms and legs. Rose's tits about tripled in size before she had Carl Jr. Man, as big as BJ's were, I could see her getting top-heavy, like Jayne Mansfield.

Life with BJ, even if it was brown bread for a while, was something I wanted to fight for. I'd be there with her the whole way, watching our baby grow. And in my heart, I actually did believe that together—Beej, the buckeye, our boy, and me—we'd make it all right.

chapter nine

I got back to Juniper High at twenty till six, just in case BJ got out of skit practice early, and sat in the dark cab of the pickup with the radio off. Jesus, I wished there was somebody to help me figure out the right way to marry her. *Not* marrying her would be the chickenshit thing to do—that much I was sure of.

I got a look inside a working radio one time—all those tubes, wires, and lights. Seemed to me like my head probably worked about the same way. Made me wish somebody could hook me up a little different, improve on my reception. Right now, for example, was a time I needed to take a deep seat, like the bull riders say: hunker down and think fast and clear.

It might help to talk to Mom. She wasn't half-bad at sorting out things. But not this time—no way. She'd bugged the hell out of me when she found the rubbers in my billfold last year. She'd have a duck if she knew that the same thing was happening to Beej and me that did to her and my ole man. "History repeats," she kept saying. "You're putting yourself in harm's way, son. I know the dangers firsthand."

And Dad wouldn't be any help, even if I could find him. He'd only lasted three weeks the last time he tried coming home. My mom was as happy as accordion music to see him, with a smile on her face like a kid on her birthday. She even started putting on red lipstick again and cooked creamed pork chops and pineapple upside-down cake. But after the first week, the smile wore down like the tread on an old tire.

When I opened the door that last night, the first thing I smelled was stale beer. It was about six o'clock, right after football practice, and Mom was crying back in their bedroom in between talking in screams. "Goddamn it, Harry, don't put us through this again! I can't take it. Get out. Just go!" Something crashed. "Oh, swell, go ahead. The football hero. Throw things. That'll make it better. That's the only thing you've ever been worth a damn at, isn't it? Throwing things." Another crash. "Well, Robbie's twice the quarterback you ever thought about being, and you don't even have the guts to face it." A crash again and a string of cuss words from him. I figured from the sounds back there that he was throwing something big, like bedroom lamps. I wanted to turn around, go back out the door, and stay gone till he sobered up. He scared the shit out of me when he got like that. But because of Mom, I couldn't. He kept yelling like a son of a bitch. I wondered what was left back there for him to break. Besides her. I had to do something.

I tried making it into a joke. "Anybody home?"

"Not for long." It was Mom, walking out of the bedroom, looking like she'd already been hit by a lamp. There was blood smeared on the side of her face, and one eye was swelled up half-closed, a bluish color. Her usual smooth, shiny brown hair had been pulled out of the rubber band at the back of her neck and was hanging down. So I was too late.

"Tell your father goodbye," she said. There was blood stuck to her teeth. Was one of the front ones missing? My stomach did a 360. "He's leaving for good, Robbie." She took a couple of uneven steps across the living room, heading for the couch. I could see her better by the light on the end table. Then I wanted to puke—puke or slug my ole man. Her face was beat up real bad.

He staggered out of the bedroom behind her, so drunk he could hardly walk. But still so goddamned big and mean-looking. And that awful empty look was back in his eyes. No wonder Mom was scared of him. I went to jelly inside. Jesus, there was something so crazy about having to fight your ole man to save your mom.

"What'd you do to her, Dad?" My voice went high like I was a kid. He didn't act like he'd heard me, just hollow-stared at the front door. He stank of beer. The pocket on his navy work shirt was torn loose, and his shirttail was pulled out on one side. His eyes, the same brown color as mine, were bugged out and bloodshot, like something inside his head was pushing against them. His fists were both clenched, like he'd slug me, too, if I said the wrong thing. And he'd done it before.

I might be able to hold my own with him now. I was in better shape and an inch taller, even though he still outweighed me by twenty pounds or more. "Shit, boy." His words were all slurry. "Nothing I do shuits this pishant mother of yours. It's hard to sit your shaddle when your goddamned woman shoots your horse out from under you." He aimed a finger and thumb in a pretend gun and took a shot back at Mom over by the couch. "You shtay right where you're at, Doreen."

I moved a step closer to her, my heart pulse pounding inside my head. I had to protect her. She was leaning against the end of the couch, not saying a word to my ole man, just pointing *her* finger at the door. There was blood all over her white blouse and splotches of it on the linoleum. "Go!" she told him, and she lifted her chin up like she still had her pride. "I haven't done a thing to you. You've managed to do it all by yourself."

His head jerked around, and his eyes went to slits. Then he tilted like he might fall over, grabbed the arm of a chair, and looked back my way, squinting, like he wondered who I was. At least he wasn't coming after me. "I ought to kick your young ass, too. What'sh the matter, boy? Cat got your tongue?"

I was afraid to say anything. *Boy.* He'd always called me that when he was drinking. Like he didn't remember my name.

He looked back at Mom. "Well, I'm going to do you a favor." He smiled with too much teeth. "My whole god-damned lifeth's been a one-way street, so I think I'll just keep walking. If you know whath's good for you, Doreen, you'll shtay out of my way." He stepped sideways toward the door, still looking back at her, not me. "Thish is the best day of my life because it'sh the last day I will take your fucking lip." It took him three tries to get the doorknob turned, and then the door opened so fast he staggered backward, then forward, and finally outside into the dark without another sound.

Cold wind blasted in through the door. One living room curtain wrapped around a stand-up lamp and crashed it to the floor. The magazine on the coffee table blew off toward the kitchen. Both windows by the door rattled in the wind, but Mom didn't move to shut it, and I didn't, either. We just stood, staring after him, me with my fists balled up in case he came back. Outside, the wind was screaming, a sound like cats fighting. Inside, the wind was freezing us. Mom's blood began to drip slower. My fists started aching from being clenched at the ready for so long.

But he didn't come back—not to get his mackinaw, his galoshes, his suitcase, nothing. He just walked out into the screaming-cats snowstorm and disappeared. When I saw he was really gone, I snapped out of it, unclenched my fists, zipped my coat, and headed for the door. "I'll find him, Mom. He'll freeze to death out there."

"Close the door, Robbie." Her voice was colder than the wind was, and mean-sounding. "Leave him be. If he froze to death, he'd be doing us a favor."

I gulped a mouthful of the cold air to clear my head, then pushed the door shut and locked it. Went over to help her by the couch. When she opened her right hand, there was a glob of blood with her tooth in it.

We didn't hear from him again, but we know he didn't freeze to death. It took a week for Mom's face to heal enough that she could go back to her flower shop. When she came home from work that first afternoon, the side window by the kitchen stoop had been pried open. His work clothes and Grandpa's broken railroad-retirement pocket watch were still in the old suitcase where he'd left them. But his scrapbook, all filled with yellowed newspaper clippings about when he'd been the football star at Juniper High, it was gone.

BJ didn't think he should get away with treating our family like that. She wanted to call Sheriff Madsen and report him for hitting Mom. But Rose said to leave well enough alone. "It's good he's gone," she said. "He resents you, Robbie." She flipped little Carl Jr. over her shoulder. "He's got to think he was the greatest ballplayer that ever was. That was as good as it ever got for him." Carl Jr. barfed, and it ran onto Rose's shoulder. She ignored it and kept on talking. "Then the war came along, he got drafted, and football ended for him. Mom says you're so much like him back then it's like he spit you out. And he hates you for it—might even hurt you, if he got enough booze in him."

I shivered in the cold of the pickup cab, remembering all that. I still wished I knew where my ole man was. Because right now, I needed him to tell me how to do what I was about to do. The temperature must have dropped ten degrees since I'd pulled up to the high school, and still no BJ. I started the motor and cut on the heat just as the double doors to the gym flew open. She came out first, lit up by the light over the door. Seeing her made my hands feel weak. Nella and Midge came right behind, darting around her like minnows in a trout stream.

Nella was cute in a redheaded, freckled, string bean–sort of way. Big smile; innocent, big eyes that filled up her face. And smart—helping-you-study-for-algebra-tests smart, I'd give her that—but bossy. And she had a problem of talking too much. Which she was doing right then, nonstop, and laughing as they headed my way, her hands waving in the air. Midge was somebody I'd think about taking out if I wasn't about to marry BJ. She'd favor Elizabeth Taylor, curves and all, if she dropped about ten pounds. A real go-getter kind of person. Not such a prude as Nella and knew how to give a guy a good time. At least, that's what Pork had heard from Mike Chase. Together, the three of them—Midge, Nella, and BJ—they were the smartest girls in the senior class. And the presidents of everything.

Right then, her friends or not, I knew all BJ wanted to do was ditch them. Which was easier said than done because they stuck to her like bark on a Christmas tree. And usually acted like they were doing me a flipping favor when she left them long enough to come with me. 'Specially Nella, whose mouth was going strong when I rolled down the pickup window and stuck out my head. "I want my woman, Nella! Let her go!"

Nella's head jerked up, and she began to run across the track to my truck. Didn't stop till she poked her head in the window. "Want to save a life?" she asked. "My battery's dead in the Jeep, and BJ said you'd give me a jump."

Great. Just great. Good luck on planning the rest of my life, with Nella around. Forty-five minutes later, by the time I'd gotten the Jeep cranked, BJ was lying down on the front seat of the pickup, the radio and the heater going. "I'm so sorry," she said as I opened the door. "There wasn't anything I could do."

I slid into the driver's seat. "It's okay," I told her. "You couldn't help it. Nella said she hoped you felt better."

BJ put her head on my lap under the steering wheel. "Beej," I said as I pulled away from the curb, "I know it's too late to talk much tonight, but I've done a lot of thinking." I gunned the motor. "This is gonna work out all right."

"Really?" She pulled her parka up over her shoulders. "I've been thinking, too. What do you think we should do?"

I knew from what Rose had taught me that a girl like BJ wouldn't want to be asked to get married in the cab of a pickup at six thirty on a Thursday night, so I decided to wait. I was steering with my left hand, running my fingers through her hair with my right. Liked the feel of her smooth hair between my fingers. "I'm taking you to the Maverick tomorrow night for dinner," I said. "I'll tell you all about it then."

She sighed. "Wow, the Maverick Supper Club. This must be serious."

I smiled. The only other time I'd blown that much money was prom night our junior year. We drove along without talking, listening to the radio, and then our song came on, "Moments to Remember."

The quiet walks, the noisy fun, the ballroom prize we almost won. We will have these moments to remember.

"Neat, huh?" I said as I slowed for the turn onto Absaraka Street. "They're playing our song."

She didn't answer. The streetlight there by a big egg-shaped rock on the corner lit up the front seat of the pickup. She was sound asleep. I stopped the truck for a minute, just let it idle as I looked down at her, feeling half-scared and half-amazed that inside BJ, my baby was growing. She looked breakable, like one of those blown-glass figurines in Totman's curio-shop window. I promised myself again that I'd take care of her, take care of *them*. As I turned the truck toward the mountains, I made myself a pledge out loud: "I won't let anything hurt them."

The moon was big and round in the sky, and I spooked a herd of antelope as I rattled over the cattle guard under the Bar Z sign. Angus, their Lab, must have tangled with a skunk again; you could even smell it with the window rolled up. I stopped the truck in front of her house and waited. Boy, she was out cold.

"You're home, sweetheart." I felt a different feeling in my heart that night, knowing she was going to be my wife. I never had called her sweetheart before.

chapter ten

B ut Beej and me didn't make the Maverick Supper Club Friday night, after all. I got reminded about Bohingi Boys' initiation after world history second period Friday morning. Pork was about to go apeshit. "You're not going to let BJ pussy whip you out of something as important as our beer run, are you?" Pork was as big as a bull, so he looked funny when he got that hurt-kid look on his face.

He had a point. The two of us, Pork and me, were the only Bohingis already eighteen and legal to buy beer up in Montana. So it was our job to get the brews for initiation that night. Drive up to Fisheagle, the cheapest near-place to get it, right after football practice, and be back in time for the fun to begin. I couldn't see I had a choice once I remembered the beer.

"Hell no," I told him and shut my notebook. "Count me in." Right away, I headed for BJ's locker—a little worried, but I figured she'd understand. I always met her there after history, anyway. We would just move the Maverick deal to Saturday night.

Jesus! I couldn't believe what a federal case she made out of it. It was the first time in my life I was actually glad

Nella was hanging around her locker next to BJ's, because it didn't go over big.

"You mean you're going out drinking with the guys instead of talking to me about you-know-what?" BJ's eyes were so surprised I had to look away for a minute, down below the edge of my letter sweater at Nella's skinny, freckled legs and the concrete floor painted gray. When I did look back at Beej, her eyes held a staring-off look identical to Mom's that night my ole man left. BJ bent over to get something out of her locker, stood back up without it, and frowned at me. Her cheeks were bright pink, a true sign of how pissed she was.

Well, I was getting pissed, too.

"I can't believe this, Rob!" She said it so loud that Pork, who was about eight lockers away, turned around, looking worried. I shook my head and gave him a thumbs-up. He nodded, slammed his locker shut, and headed off down the hall.

"Geez, BJ. Don't bust a gut!" So Nella wouldn't hear, I moved close to her. "We can go tomorrow night. Saturday they have a band. It's The Belltones." I tried putting my arm around her, but she pulled away. "It's my senior year, my last initiation ever. I *gotta* go. Besides, they're counting on Pork and me for the beer."

"Is there any logical reason you can't just go up to Fisheagle, get the beer, and then come back and get me?" She didn't whisper, so Nella was looking back and forth, trying to figure what the shit was going on—which was none of her business to start with. "What could possibly be wrong with that?" I hated BJ's voice when she got all know-it-all. "Then you could look after your precious fraternity brothers and me, too, couldn't you?"

Nella interrupted. "You guys better argue later. BJ, we're about to be late for English. You know Miss Emory."

"I'll risk it," BJ said. "You go on." They must have sent some girl-code message, because Nella shrugged and left, which I wished she hadn't done, because I couldn't come up with the right words to tell Beej why it was I absolutely had to go with the Bohingis this one last time. And I couldn't believe she didn't see my point. Dad had warned me how quick a woman can turn on you if you don't do what she wants you to. Like one time when Mom wouldn't give him money for booze. "Doreen," he'd said, "I honestly don't believe you'd piss on me if I was burning to death."

After Nella left, BJ whirled on me like a coiled-up rattlesnake. "So," she said, folding both her arms under her breasts—which were already growing, from what I could tell. It was hard to concentrate when she had on that blue sweater and her crossed arms under them. "It's the same old thing: you're going out with the guys, leaving me to get through this horrible, cruddy day all by myself."

The class buzzer rang loud, right over our heads. Made me jump a foot. But BJ didn't move, just frowned and hugged her arms tighter. "Then you'll come and chat with me about it when it suits your convenience?"

Mr. Blotnick—the Ostrich, we called him—poked his head on his long neck around the corner of the chem-lab door. "Don't you two have places you're supposed to be?" The way his Adam's apple bobbed up and down when he talked, it was hard not to stare. Talk about a man who could use a good weight program.

"Yes, sir." BJ used her ice-water voice. "We were *just* going." She slammed her locker door and left before I even realized she was leaving. Didn't say one more damn word to me, just stomped down the hall into Miss Emory's room, two doors down. I was so royally pissed that I didn't stop her. Maybe Dad had a point about women; you couldn't let 'em push you around.

Pork was stripped down to his Fruit of the Looms when I got to the locker room to dress for PE. "You're not going to fink out, are you?" He still looked worried.

"Hell no." I unbuttoned my shirt. "Nothing would make me miss our last initiation together." I meant it, too.

"Good man." He bent over to pull his socks off, and I looked away quick. With the sock off, his left foot gave me the heebie-jeebies. No little toe. It had been cut off by a thrown pocketknife when Pork was in the third grade. His brother, Moose, had made the bad mumblety-peg throw. I waited till Pork got both tennis shoes back on before I looked at him again. His back had dark hair all over it. To me, Pork was like what a real man ought to be. I could never figure why girls didn't go for him.

By the end of that day, I got the message that BJ wasn't the only one against the Bohingi initiation. Last thing Coach said before we left the gym was, "I hear the Bohingis are initiating tonight. If you boys know what's good for you, you won't break training for some dumb high school fraternity." He put an arm around my shoulder. Coach always smelled of liniment—clean, so different from my ole man—and he always shaved. "Rob, you have a lot at stake next week." His most serious Sergeant Friday voice. "Ed Delaney, one of the assistant coaches down at the university, is a friend of mine. He's coming to watch you work out next week, may even stay to scout the homecoming game. It could make or break your chances for a scholarship."

"Yes, sir," I told him, looking him almost in the eyes. "I'll keep straight." But I didn't mean it. Grown-ups lost touch with stuff like that. I figured a good party would loosen me up, help me play better. All day long, though, I'd gotten madder and madder about how shitty BJ had treated me when I was about to give up everything for her. So I didn't go back to her locker, and she sure as hell didn't show up at mine. Was it going to be a fight every time I wanted to go out with one of my buddies? By the time football practice was over, I was ready to head out, down a few brews, and forget the whole mess.

Pork beat me out of the locker room, was sitting in the driver's seat of his green '56 Chevy, reading *Popular Mechanics* when I came out. It was only four thirty. Coach was good that way—gave us short practices on the Fridays when we didn't have games. Pork's Chevy was his joy and pride. He'd worked two summers stacking Dixie Cups at the Creamery to get the car money. Soon as he'd bought it, he raked the back end, bought an *oogah* horn, and pinstriped both sides in this shiny purple color. He looked relieved when I came out. "Sorry," I said. "I had to take a leak."

He got out of the Chevy and came over to climb into my pickup, which had more room for hauling beer. "I've decided to trade my car for a '55 Bel Air. Been reading about it. A needle valve on the carburetor, one sixty-two under the hood—talk about acceleration. It's gonna be one vintage automobile."

I grinned at him. He knew why, too, and grinned back, sheepish like. Every week or two, since he was a kid, Pork would fall in love with another automobile. God, I knew him so well! If a guy can love another guy the right way, that's how I loved Pork. Not like a cornholer or anything. A comfortable feeling, like real friends.

I started the pickup, looking at him from the corner of my eye. Six three, with arms like tree limbs. Same height as me but outweighed me by thirty, forty pounds. The guy you want blocking in the line ahead of you every Friday night. Already going a little bald on the front part of his head. He was the owner of some of the biggest zits I'd ever seen. "Boils," Mom had called them. A prairie dog colony all over his cheeks that had started growing there in about the eighth grade. When Pork got bored, he'd squeeze one, and if he didn't like you, he might aim it your way. It made the girls nervous. Maybe that was why they bad-mouthed Pork. He was also the best-hung guy I knew, which was the explanation for why we guys called him Pork. His real name was Claude Ramseur. Pork got a kick out of it when girls began calling him Pork, too, because he knew how grossed out they'd be if they found out what kind of compliment they were paying him. BJ had an idea of it, I think, and tried to worm it out of me once. But I couldn't tell her; it was Pork's personal secret.

First thing Pork did when he climbed into my pickup that day was change my radio to KWWO. I'd expected it. He only listened to country music. He had on his snakeskin cowboy boots, a Western shirt with pearl snap buttons, and his usual chaw of Red Man in his pocket.

The round trip to Fisheagle took about an hour and a half, with the buying of the beer included, but it went fast. We sang as loud as we could every time Hank Williams came on: "Your Cheatin' Heart," "Honky Tonkin'"—good music. Every truck we passed, Pork leaned out the window and gave them the jerk-jerk elbow signal to blow their horn or whistle. Pork and me could kick back like kids when the mood hit us. Probably because we'd known each other so long. We had a lawn-mowing service when we were eleven, mowed four lawns every week to save up for our Louisville Sluggers. Ordered our Green Hornet decoder rings together, too, even earlier than that. What were we? Six, seven? The year after that, we set a new record at Boy Scout camp, singing "99 Bottles of Beer on the Wall" start to finish two hundred times before the counselors held pillows over our heads.

And it was me Pork had called our junior year, a hint of crying in his voice. "Oh God, Rob. I just hit Elvis with the Creamery truck, his whole back end. He's hurting real bad. Would you get out here to the Armory fast as you can and help me get him to the vet?" They'd had to cut Elvis's right back leg off, but the other three kept on running fine. Both Pork and me take credit for the fact that ole Elvis is chasing cars again, just one leg shy of most dogs.

Even appreciating Pork like I did, BJ stayed in the back of my mind. What in the hell was I supposed to do now? Maybe I could talk to Pork about it, but I wasn't sure that was a great idea. First, Pork didn't know shit about girls, and second, you had to get him in the right mood.

When we crossed the state line into Montana, he began looking for Indians in every car we passed. When he saw his first one, he flipped him the bone and then died laughing. So far, it didn't seem like the best time to tell him about BJ. We had to drive thirty miles through the Cheyenne

Reservation to get to Fisheagle. Scared the shit out of me, him flipping off more Indians. "I'm feeling like General Custer," I told him. "You flip off the wrong one, they'll cut my gizzard out, too."

"That's the fun of it." He stuffed a chaw of Red Man inside his lip. "It keeps life interesting."

"You hate Indians, Pork?"

"Aw, hell no," he said. "I just like to lower the odds." His smile was crooked. He was teasing me. "Walk on the wild side."

I thought about how Pork *did* like danger as we rode along. Me, I wanted the odds the other way. When Coach played me at safety in the Gillette game, and their big fullback, Arthur Treakler, came charging down on me, I almost peed in my pants. I could have tackled him. Instead, I slowed down just enough to have a good excuse not to, and he ran past me into the end zone. Motivated me to make sure we scored again. Otherwise, I'd be the one who lost us the game. Pork wouldn't have done that. He wasn't afraid of much.

So maybe what had happened to me with BJ wouldn't even bother him. Who else could I talk to? I had just made up my mind to tell him about it when, out of nowhere, he torpedoed that, asking me, "You ever talk BJ into going down on you?"

I braked to miss a jackrabbit, took a minute to think what to say back. What went on between Beej and me was our own personal business. He knew that. "Why you asking, Pork?" I stretched my back out and tried not to seem interested.

"Just curious." He scratched under his chin. Pork had a way of shaving his face that left his neck not shaved. No wonder it itched. "Mike Chase was home from Laramie last weekend. He's got Midge doing it." Pork yawned, stretched. "Big college man and all. Said it was his solution to DSB since Midge is trying to save her cunt for her wedding night." Pork shrugged. "Says it's the next best thing to banging her."

"DSB?" I cut the radio down. "What's DSB?"

Pork exploded laughing. "An old cock hound like yourself, you probably never have suffered from DSB." He lowered his voice. "It is the dreaded disease, Deadly Sperm Buildup. Untreated, it leads to yellow jaundice, fits, and horrible death by strangulation." He started fake-choking himself with both hands, and his laugh went high. Pork's laugh was weird.

A black horse in the pasture next to the road started running inside the fence like it wanted to race us. Pork began cracking the knuckles on his right hand, one at a time. Which drove Mom up a tree. "Me," he said—crack, crack, crack; then moving over to his left hand—"me, I'm getting pretty sick of just jerking off." Crack, crack, crack.

"Lexie might go down on you," I said, "if you feed her enough beer and tell her you love her. Or you could always pay one of Lu-Lu's girls." I turned to look at him. "Shit, Pork, when did you start getting horny?"

"I'm not horny. Mike just got me to wondering about you and BJ. Going together all these years, I figure you'd worked something out. Problem is, the kind of girl you'd want to marry, somebody smart as BJ, she's not going to give it away till she's got you hog-tied and kneeling at the altar." He cracked some more knuckles and reached to turn up the radio again. "I just figured you might have come up with . . . Well, let's call it a *creative solution*, like Mike has."

"Jesus H. Christ!" Something slipped in place in my head. "Pork, have you got a woman? You son of a bitch." I punched him on the shoulder. "You're fishing for information. I'll be goddamned! You've been holding out on me!"

When Pork got embarrassed, the big round tip at the end of his nose wrinkled down. His smile went shy, a look I hadn't seen on him since grade school. "Shit." He scratched his chin again. "Well, she's older—couple years older. New in town. Works nights down at the Creamery. Nobody's put the bad mouth on me yet." He shrugged. "And frankly, Rob, she's offering me her little pepper pot." He smiled big. "But Ramseur men don't shoot blanks. I've got, what—ten nieces and nephews already? I want to take her up on it, but I don't want to end up with a bun in the oven, ruin my life over a piece of tail, if you know what I mean."

Boy, did I ever know. I slowed down for the traffic light at Fisheagle.

Pork shrugged. "You being the original ladies' man, I figured you might share a few tricks of the trade."

He was cracking his knuckles again. No wonder it bugged Mom.

I downshifted at the stoplight. "Yeah," I told him. "It is a problem. You can always pull out or use a rubber, but nothing's a hundred percent." Shit, I couldn't believe he was talking to me about the very thing I was sweating blood over. "Anyway," I said, "here we are. Let's get the beer before the sun goes down."

chapter eleven

Fisheagle was two grocery stores, a gas station, and six bars. The kind of place you get out of before dark. When we pulled out of town with some candy to eat and the back of the truck full of beer, the sun looked like the inside of a hard-boiled egg sitting on top of the mountain.

My stomach felt nervous as we crossed the reservation— little hut-houses; horses with their heads hanging and ribs sticking out; mangy, scrawny dogs lying in the dust in the front yards; beat-up cars; rusted refrigerators sitting on the side of the road; grass all brown and worn down. It made me feel guilty, like it was my fault the Indians had to live that way. So I was glad when we crossed the state line back into Wyoming and left it all behind. Pork didn't bring up the girl questions again. I was glad about that. The Hershey's bars hit the spot. Male ones, Pork said, because they had nuts. I ate three, but the funny feeling I'd had in my stomach all day wouldn't go away. I tried reading the Burma-Shave signs along the road. *If your face is sad . . . and way too rough . . .*

"Hey," Pork asked, "is it true Indians don't have to shave?"

I slowed at the crossroads with the beat-up LIVE BAIT sign. The right turn went to Tomahawk Lake, the left turn back toward the mountains. "I've heard it said," I told him. "Don't know for sure." I turned left, began looking for the road to Danny Owensby's. "Do you see the cutoff yet?" His dad had a mountain cabin out near Story that he let us use. Mr. Owensby was a hunched-over, kind of Ed Sullivan–shaped person who really understood boys. "I'll let you use it once a year," he'd said, "to save you guys from yourselves." But the road to the cabin was easy to miss.

I wondered where BJ was, wished I could do something to make the tight feeling in my gut go away. Like breathing through my mouth to keep from smelling shit in an out-house, but it was too complicated.

Out of the corner of my eye, I saw a coyote disappear into the aspen trees there at the foot of the mountain. You didn't see many coyotes, just heard them yipping off in the hills when you were hunting. Seeing a coyote felt like seeing a ghost. Jesus, I needed a beer or something.

I looked away from the aspens, out west toward the mountains where Pork was staring. The sun was gone now. All that was left was melting colors in the sky, like crayons when you leave them on the radiator, which I knew about from my own personal experience. First yellow, then orange and red; finally—just before it disappeared—the sky got all pink, the color of BJ's cheeks today when she'd been so pissed. Shit. Why couldn't I leave it for one frigging night?

The sky was dark purple when I found the long drive to Mr. Owensby's cabin. Pork had cut the radio back on and begun singing again. The tall black pine trees lining the road kept out the light like somebody had unplugged the stars. The smell of the trees cleared my head the way Mentholatum does. That many trees all crowded together made it cold and lonely feeling.

A bunch of the Bohingis were standing in front of the cabin around a tub of ice they had ready for the beer. They cheered when they saw our lights, ran to meet the truck, and followed us in. Pork and me were two popular guys at that moment.

Even with the rocky start, it turned out to be one great night. We put analgesic balm on the new guys' balls, and when they got through rolling around in pain from that, we made them drink some God-awful concoction made out of tobacco, Coke, a little piss, and a lot of hot pepper. While they puked, we sat around telling dirty jokes and chugging the beer. It just got better and better. I laughed so hard I completely forgot how fucked up my world was—at least for a while.

At about two thirty, when the beer ran out, Pork was so drunk he found a bottle of Danny's mom's perfume in a dresser drawer and tried drinking it, which made him remind me of somebody, but I couldn't remember who. Till I did. "It's Miss Cantor!" I yelled, pointing at him. "Pork smells like the girls' guidance counselor." He grabbed me, started slugging my shoulder hard, then harder, but I wouldn't stop. "Pork smells like Miss Cantor. Pork smells like Miss Cantor . . ."

Next morning, I woke up thrashing around in my sleeping bag after the damnedest dream. I'd been sinking in quicksand. BJ, Pork, my ole man, and Coach had been standing around this pit, watching me suck under, but nobody would pull me out. When I'd finally gotten my head cleared, I figured I might have been better off in the quicksand. God, I was hungover, and there was a big purple bruise on my throwing arm where Pork had been slugging me. I stretched it over and over, trying to work out the soreness. The cabin only had one bathroom, and I didn't feel like jumping in the stream with Pork, so I sat in the kitchen and looked through Danny's *Playboy* till it was my turn in the shower. "Hey, Pork!" I yelled when he came dripping back into the cabin. "Maybe you ought to write the *Playboy* adviser about DSB."

He slugged me again on my poor aching arm.

By the time Ted Lackman said the bathroom was clear, the hot water was long gone. I probably needed a cold shower, anyway, to knock some sense back in me. I got a look at myself in the mirror over the bathroom sink when I stepped out of the stall, and it shocked the hell out of me. Because I was looking into my own ole man's blood-streaked eyes. Jesus, was I acting like him, too?

My heart started pounding in my chest like it had to get out. I knew then I had to get to BJ as fast as I could. For some reason, I felt scared shitless.

I got Ted to give Pork a ride back to Juniper, then climbed into my truck and headed for the Bar Z. I stopped in Big Horn at the Esso station for a buck's worth of gas; got my aftershave out of my glove compartment; and took it in the men's room, where the light was better for combing my hair. I slapped on a lot of aftershave so I at least wouldn't smell like my ole man. It seemed like I didn't look so much like him in that light. The rubber machine was on the wall by the urinal. I reached in my pocket, automatic-like, for change to resupply myself—then remembered. I wouldn't be needing rubbers anymore. I got excited thinking that we could do it now without any rubber between us.

I asked Mr. Suttle—*Lloyd* was the name stitched on his uniform shirt—if I could borrow his phone inside the station. The pay phone outside had been broken as long as I could remember. As I dialed BJ, I got an eyeful of Miss October on the wall calendar hanging there. She had a yellow see-through scarf wrapped around her ass and a sideways view of her long banana tits.

Mrs. Bonniface answered the phone, came back after a long time to say BJ didn't want to talk to me. Miss October's ass blurred in front of my eyes. That awful flapping-bird panic came up in my chest again. It was hard to make my voice sound half-normal.

"Mrs. Bonniface," I said, "this is real important. I *need* to talk to her. I'm going to come anyway, if it's all right with you. I'm already in Big Horn."

"Suit yourself," she said. "She's on her way to Standing Elk's." Her voice moved away from the phone. "You may be able to catch her if you hurry."

"Thanks." I felt my heart quiet down in my chest. "And Mrs. Bonniface?"

"Yes, Rob?"

"I'll see you soon, then."

chapter twelve

eemed like it took twice as long as usual to get from
Big Horn to the Bar Z. Big dirty clouds were hanging over Mount Quandary. Even though Beej was
wrong for sure about the Bohingi Boys' deal, I had this
crummy feeling it was my fault. I'd feel better when we got
it straightened out.

Just before I entered Tongue River Canyon, where the
paved road turned into dirt, I passed Preacher's Rock, a great
big pile of giant boulders sticking fifty, seventy-five feet up
in the air. They say some preacher a long time ago burned
words on the flat-sided stone there with a smoking candle:
The wages of sin is death. It was pretty faded, but you could
still read it. I licked my lips; they were sticking to my teeth.
A bad, tinny taste. Maybe it was just the hangover. I was
glad when I came out the end of the canyon into the valley
where the Bar Z was.

It was spitting snow—a light, dry snow like the talc
we put on our feet when we wrapped before a game. The
curly red backs of the Herefords in the pasture there by the
road were getting whiter, too. Lots of dead grass sticking up
through the snow that brought to mind my ole man's face
when he hadn't shaved, gray-brown stubble. Not enough
snow to cover up the grass, but enough to make things

look cold and unfriendly. Usually, I liked being alone, but a deserted feeling came upon me in my chest. If it got much worse, I'd need an iron lung to breathe.

The closer I got to the ranch, the lower the clouds dropped, till the whole sky seemed balanced right on top of Mount Quandary, as dark and bruised as my throwing arm. I flexed it a couple of times. It was stiffer now than it had been that morning. I rolled down the window. It smelled like snow. Rolled up the window and tried to make better time, but the bumpy road beat the hell out of my truck. There was no antelope herd where they usually hung out, in the field by the old Franklin place. A bad storm was blowing in. Gusts were hitting the pickup harder now. I had to work to keep it in the ruts and hold the road. The phone line, looped along beside the road, was whipping around like crazy.

Dad got saved once by a telephone line like that. He and Cy Gentry were elk hunting up on Butler Flats. Cy's Jeep broke down just as a big front moved in. They waited out the snowstorm in their sleeping bags inside the Jeep. By morning, the snow was so deep they couldn't push open the doors, so they had to climb out the windows. Dad said everything was covered with snow: fence posts, rivers, rocks, even some of the trees. The only things they could see besides the mountains and snow were the tops of some big trees and one phone line running across the valley. So they followed the line down on snowshoes to get out, the way you'd follow a stream if you were lost.

"I'm telling you the truth," Dad said to me. "We like to froze to death. My fingers went blacker than tar paper, and Cy lost two. Without them telephone lines, I wouldn't have made it down, and you wouldn't be here today, sonny boy."

Dad hadn't told me many stories, so I never forgot that one about the phone line saving him. I was betting that empty feeling in my chest would go away fast if he showed up and acted like a real dad. He'd walk up on our front stoop, put his arm around my shoulder like Coach, and say, "Well, son, I see you've got yourself in one hell of a mess. Let's see what your ole man can do to help you out." He'd even understand how hard it was for me, since he'd gone through the same thing back in 1939, when he and Mom had Rose.

The peak of Mount Quandary was white now. Out over the mountains, dark clouds were still boiling. I downshifted by the scraggly pines at the Bonnifaces' first gate. Twenty or thirty cows were hanging out there, around a box-shaped haystack, their breath making little puffs of smoke in the cold. Then it came again—that lonely, cold, hard-to-breathe feeling. Damn.

I cut the heater up a notch. Good heater; it helped a little. The new drift fence on the other side of the gate must have been there Thursday night when I brought BJ home from Doc Justice's. Had that only been two days ago? I hadn't seen it in the dark.

I turned under the big poles over their second gate, the huge iron Bar Z brand swinging in the wind above me. The cattle guard clanged like hell, as usual. Then I passed the double hills to the right, where the Bonnifaces' family cemetery was. I wanted to hike up there some time and have a look. I didn't see BJ as I crossed the bridge over Quandary Creek and was just as glad. I decided on the spot to go up to the ranch house and wait for her there.

Going to Standing Elk's shack gave me the creeps. His beady little dried-up raisin eyes sank so deep in his head that he had to lift his chin to see you, which he didn't do very much, because he seemed to have some kind of Indian sixth sense. He knew things you were damn sure you'd never told him and never wanted him to know in the first place.

His three crows—BJ called them ravens—hung out in the top of a cottonwood tree by his shack. Better than a burglar alarm. You couldn't get within a quarter of a mile of the place before they took off, cawing and raising hell. BJ swore to me that Standing Elk talked to birds and they understood. Once, she saw him call in a pair of eagles from where they nested on Tomahawk Bluff with a high-pitched eagle scream from out the back of his throat.

I didn't exactly believe the eagle story, but there was something uncomfortable and different about Standing Elk and his whole situation on the Bar Z. His skin color, for one thing, wasn't like any other Indian I knew—too light and too thin. And where he lived was odd. Nobody else I knew let Indians live rent-free on their ranch. As particular a businessman as Mr. Bonniface was, it didn't make sense. The rest of the Cheyennes and the Crow Indians I knew about lived up on the reservations with their own kind and kept to themselves. They even got free money from the government to buy iceboxes and washing machines and stuff. Standing Elk wasn't better off living at the Bar Z. So why did he stay? Maybe because his mother, Bird, had lived there her whole life. BJ said she was an old-timey medicine woman, so good at it that white people came to her when nothing else got them well. I could see a point to *that*, now.

I slowed the truck to a crawl to give BJ plenty of time to get to Standing Elk's without me. But she must have waited for me, because when I drove around the last bend in the road, there she was in a bright-yellow ski parka and a purple headscarf I'd never seen before. Casper colors.

All of a sudden, I couldn't think of what to say to her. My heart started pounding like I'd run a mile. I downshifted and pulled off to a side road a couple of yards into the trees by the river so we'd have some privacy. She was walking my way, so I rolled down the window.

"Fancy meeting you here," she said in a shitty little know-it-all voice. "It's only lunchtime. I figured you'd still be out cold at Danny's."

The scarf made her eyes look purple blue. Seeing her—even mad at me—still made me hot. "Get in," I told her. "We've got to talk." It surprised me how calm my voice sounded.

"What's wrong with talking right here?" She folded her arms. Her mouth was a thin blue line. The wind jerked out the ends on her purple scarf and snapped them behind her. She had to be freezing. She unfolded her arms and stuck the scarf ends back under her collar.

"You're turning blue," I said, "and I'm rolling up *my* window before I freeze." I started rolling.

"Big Bohingi Boy afraid of a little cold?" The wind tore her scarf loose again. She shivered, so I figured I'd at least get her in the pickup. Another blast shook the cab as she walked around the front of the truck to open the door on the passenger side. I picked up some cigars Pork had left on the seat and shoved them into the glove box, along with my church key and a package of cherry bombs. When I had the seat clear, I stuck out my hand to haul her in. She was so short she had trouble with the big step up into the cab. She looked at my hand but didn't take it, heaved herself up on the door handle, and swung in on the door—hard as hell on my hinges, but I figured it wasn't the time to say so. She got herself settled on the far side of the seat, about as far away as she could get, then turned and stared at me.

"You get any closer to the door handle," I said, "it'll grow into your side."

She gave me a disgusted look, folded her arms over her chest again. So far, joking wasn't working. That tin taste came back in my mouth.

"New coat?" I smiled. "You look like a canary. Add in that scarf, and you're ready to cheer for the enemy next weekend."

"It's Mom's," she said. "And right now, I *feel* like cheering for Casper."

She was beginning to piss me off again. "God, BJ. What's with this ice-woman treatment?" I reached out to cut off the ignition, then saw how cold she still looked and decided to leave the heater running a little longer. I didn't have a whole lot of gas left.

"What's wrong," she said, "is, I don't want to wait till tonight to talk this over. I've been sick all morning, and I've got to make some decisions. Mom heard me throwing up again and wants to haul me in to Doc. If you have anything to say to me, please just say it now."

"Oh hell," I said. "I wanted to do it right for you, but I'll tell you now. I don't think we have any choice about it. I love the hell out of you when you're not acting like such a bi . . . when you're not acting dumb." The biggest gust of wind yet shook the truck. A low limb on a tree above us scraped the roof of my cab.

She looked up at the tree. Then her head snapped back my way. "Oh, that's great," she said. "Now I'm a dumb bitch because I'm not arranging my life to fit your fraternity's time schedule."

"Hold on. Let me finish. I don't want you going through this alone. He's my kid, too, you know." I had a perfect idea. I leaned over her to the glove box, opened it, and pulled out one of Pork's White Owls, peeled off the cellophane, slipped the band off, and reached for her left hand. She let me take it, so I pulled off her purple mitten. Her fingers were freezing. I held them a minute between my hands to warm them up, then slipped the cigar band onto her ring finger. It was a little loose, but it stayed on okay.

"BJ, honey," I said, surprised my voice was creaky, like there was a frog in my throat, "will you marry me and be my wife?"

She stared like she couldn't believe what I was saying. The back of her left fist went up to her mouth. Tears started seeping out of her eyes, making her pink cheeks wet and shiny. Sometimes, BJ could look more like a doll than a girl. She stared at the White Owl ring, then up at me. "You mean that?" she whispered, all the bitch gone out of her voice. "But, Rob, how could we manage it?"

"I already talked to Mr. Quackenbush. He'll let me work overtime as many hours as I want, after football. It won't be easy, but you could work till the baby's born, and I'll get a full-time job after I graduate. We could do it, Beej."

She cocked her head, looking at me like she saw a brand-new person. "You're really serious, aren't you? You'd give up college and fraternities and football and scholarships—all that for me?" She moved toward me, keeping her eyes on my face like she thought I was the best and most wonderful boy in the whole US of A.

About then, I agreed with her. I hadn't put together a list of everything I'd be giving up to get married. "Oh, the hell with college," I said. "We can make it fine." I cut off the engine. The tank was below the quarter mark, and I'd need that much to get home.

BJ's face was all hopeful again. "Have you thought about how we'd do it?" She wiped the tears off her cheek with the back of her mitten. I reached over and helped her with my thumb. Her face was an icicle.

"I'm sorry to cut off the heater, but I'm getting pretty low on gas."

She didn't seem to care about the heater. "Have you really thought this through? What do we tell our folks? Where will we live? How do we get married? When do we tell them? Stuff like that."

I shrugged, noticed again how tight my throwing arm was. "No, but those are just things to work out. I'm not looking forward to telling your dad; I know that much. Maybe we just ought to go ahead and get it over with today."

She rubbed her nose with her mittened hand, staring down at the ring on the other one. "I'd like to get it over with, too," she said, "but this isn't exactly the way he'd approve of our doing it. I mean, if we decide to get married for sure, he'll want hard answers, a real ring. He's a stickler for things like that."

"He may take it better than you think. You know he thinks a lot of me. He might even be glad you're not leaving him and going to Wellesley. He'd be getting his own grand-kid a lot sooner than he probably expected. Heck"—I felt myself get a little excited at the idea—"there might even be a place for us here at the ranch."

She didn't look very hopeful. Then I thought of another thing. "BJ, I know a place we can stay. I bet Mom would let us have Rose's old room at my house. We could have the whole upstairs to ourselves, to start out with. She might even let you do flowers in the shop or drive the delivery truck until the baby comes. Mom loves babies. How's that for hard facts for your dad?"

"I don't know, Rob. I just don't know. I mean, I've been raised differently than you. I've never even had a real job. Your mother's great, but I think I'd have trouble living with her." New tears rolled down her cheeks. "I was really looking forward to college." She took off her right mitten and began twisting the cigar band.

"I know it's not perfect," I said. I could see my breath, so I started the engine again. Maybe BJ'd loan me a dollar to get a little more gas in Big Horn on the way home. "But we've got to start somewhere. Just say yes, and we'll work it all out to suit you."

She reached her hands out to the heater and smiled. Jesus, it felt good to see her looking happy again. "Well, okay," she said, like she was trying out the idea. "It does feel right, Rob, doesn't it? Yes . . . yes . . . yes . . ." Her eyes squeezed shut, she smiled so big.

I slid from behind the wheel and wrapped her up in my arms, unzipped the front of her coat and buried my head down inside it, kissing her neck and sucking on her collarbone, which was lots warmer than her mouth. My arm stopped hurting, and whatever had been stuck in my gut since yesterday loosened up.

She smelled like fresh air and hay, and I got so hot for her that I couldn't get my coat open fast enough. I felt her breasts grow bigger as I pulled up her sweater and unfastened her bra to get down to bare skin. God, I wanted her so much.

"BJ," I said, "if you'll loan me a dollar for gas, we can keep the car running, and"—I chewed on her earlobe, whispered in her ear—"this time we won't even need a rubber."

chapter thirteen

I t wasn't that great without the rubber. Her mind kept wandering off the whole time we did it. Once, when the wind belted the cab extra hard, she jerked away from me and looked out the window. Cornflake-size snow was falling out of the sky. "I really want to get to Standing Elk's before this settles in," she said. "I think he might be able to help us."

I came fast, anyway. The real feel of her just was too much. Right away, she got busy cleaning herself up: straightening out bra straps, tucking her sweater back in her jeans. Then she zipped her coat and opened the truck door. By the time I'd gotten back in my jeans and buttoned my jacket up, she was halfway across the big dead tree that crossed the creek like a bridge.

She waited for me on the other side. The tree had been there so long the bark was all rubbed off, so it was slippery to walk on. Still, it beat the hell out of going clear back to the road and crossing the bridge there, then a forty-minute hike back up the draw to Standing Elk's shack. My knees wobbled when I stepped out over the water. Quandary Creek was deep and wide —ten to fifteen feet across, maybe. At least it moved quiet there, didn't roar under you like it did up on Tomahawk Bluff. I acted like it was no big deal, but

I was thinking you couldn't live but a minute if you fell in, as cold and deep as the water was that day.

She gave me a good smile when I got to the other side, reached out for my hand. The cigar band crinkled in my fingers. She hadn't put her mitten back on that hand, wrinkled her nose up when she saw me notice. "You think I'm going to cover up my brand-new engagement ring just because of a little cold?"

I wished I had her a real one.

"Come on," she said. "Let's head out. We'll take the longer trail by the river and miss the stud pasture."

The narrow trail by the river wasn't wide enough to walk next to her, so I walked behind the first fifteen minutes, picturing in my mind her tight little ass as it twitched along under the yellow coat. The great big pine trees along the path blocked out so much of the light and wind that it was hard to tell what the storm was doing. No sound but the crunch of sticks under our feet and the whoosh, whoosh, whoosh of the river.

She turned around to wait for me in a clearing. The yellow coat slayed me. "You really do look like a canary!" I yelled at her.

"What?" She put her hand up to her ear. "The river's too loud." She stood out from everything gray and green, lit up in the clearing like she was in a spotlight.

A big, flat, shiny gray rock stretched from the trail out into the river. I caught up with her and followed her to the end of the rock where it stuck out over the water. "Isn't this place just magic, Rob? I come here to think. I love the way the river surrounds me." She took a real deep breath, let it out slow. "When I'm out here, I feel a part of it all, and nothing's ever as bad as it seems back at the house." She blew her bangs up off her forehead. "Standing Elk says the Great Spirit whispers in the wind and water. So loud and so quiet all at once." She smiled a faraway, talking-to-herself smile. "I always feel a million times better on this rock."

I stood behind her, looking over her head at the stream. It was grayish green, too, the colors of the trees and sky mixed together. I pulled her up against me, my arms hanging over her shoulders, and rested my chin on her purple head scarf. The smell of the pines and the sound of the river smoothed out something inside me. I could see why she liked it there.

"I've been wondering," she said after a while, "whether there's any way I can get out of being pregnant. Like in Sweden, you can just get an abortion if you're not ready to have a baby. I wrote Trina Gumpert when I got back to the house—you remember her? That cute little blonde that moved to Denver after our freshman year? I told her I had a friend who was in trouble, that I was trying to help out. You can find people to do things like that in big cities."

"BJ!" I spun her around to face me. "I already thought about that idea and decided it's a bad one. You can get yourself messed up real bad doing something stupid like that. People get killed having abortions. Besides, it's against the law."

She smiled as if I was making way too big a deal of the abortion idea. When she turned back around to look at the river, I got a crackly feeling in my head, like somebody talking too far away on a phone line wanted to tell me something important.

"Believe me," she said, laughing, "I'm not going to do anything stupid. The last thing I want to do is die." She stopped laughing. "Truth is, I guess it's the last thing we all do, isn't it?"

"Jesus, that is not funny. I don't want you to *talk* like this." I was straining to think through the static in my brain. "You wouldn't *really* do something dumb like have an abortion, would you?"

She snuggled closer to me. "Of course not. Don't worry. I never stay in a tight spot too long. There's always a way out." She raised her chin and looked up at me. I kissed the end of her nose. Like kissing a Popsicle with no taste.

"Listen to the river, Rob. It *is* like God whispering, isn't it?"

"It sure feels more like He's here than at Emmanuel Lutheran." The sun went behind a cloud. The sky darkened, then brightened as clouds floated over the sun. "This is such a weird day, BJ. One minute, it's dark and snowy; then, look—the sun's shining up there again behind the snow clouds. The weather can't make up its mind."

"You notice things more than most guys," she said. "And you're right. It's unreal, isn't it?" She let out such a big, happy sigh that she got an inch shorter under my chin. "I can't believe we're really getting married."

We stood leaned-together for a long time, like two tent-poles; the sun coming and going; the river whoosh, whoosh, whooshing around us. I felt her God-feeling, my belly going peaceful, all the static drained out of my head.

Then I felt her catch her breath. Across the river was a big, beefy eight-point buck standing like a statue, looking straight at us. It took me a minute to realize he was a deer, not an elk or a moose—he was that big. I froze. So did BJ. I couldn't believe he wasn't running, because he had to have seen us. You could see his breath in the cold and smell something wild and gamy from across the river. My heart was hammering; I wondered if he could hear that.

It felt close to a miracle, the three of us in the funny sunlight with the sound of God in the river. He didn't seem the least bit afraid. Just stared, twitched his long ears, stared again. His eyes were shiny, dark, and curious.

Finally, after what seemed like about five minutes, he put his head down in the river and sucked up some water. Then, as magically as he'd come, he turned and walked back into the trees. For a minute, it was like he hadn't even been there.

"You're ruining me," I whispered in BJ's ear. "Time was, all I'd want was Dad's .30-06. That was some kind of rack on him. Now you've got me seeing God in rivers and deers."

"I don't think I'm making you *be* any way," she said, turning around to face me. She kissed me down around the second button on my jacket. "I just think you let yourself be who you really are when you're with me instead of trying to be some jerk like Pork wants . . ." She stopped talking and stared at me. "Gosh, Rob, I didn't realize all you had on was a jean jacket. I bet you're freezing. Come on. Let's hurry and get to Standing Elk's. He'll have a fire." She turned and ran up the path.

"It's okay!" I yelled at her back, but I was getting cold. I blew on my hands, had even thought about trying to borrow that mitten she wasn't wearing, but I decided I'd feel too stupid. I took off up the path after her.

We hiked a good ten minutes more along the river trail. I thought a lot in that little bit of time, the crazy sun still coming and going. She was right, as usual—about God, and the river, and even about me. The inside Me would never want to blow away that buck. I had a feeling I'd remember that day forever, but I was too glad to have the marriage thing settled to wonder why.

chapter fourteen

When we'd made it across the pasture and hit the path through the trees to Standing Elk's place, his damn birds started cawing like hell. He was waiting for us by the campfire in his dirt front yard. He had on a wrinkled turquoise cowboy shirt and faded jeans with a big black leather belt and silver buckle. No coat or hat, but he didn't look cold. Same skinny gray braids, and he had a knife in his right hand with a hunk of meat on it.

Something cooking smelled so damn good that it healed my hungover stomach. All of a sudden, I was starved. He took the last bite of whatever was on his knife, chewed it slowly, and watched us come closer.

BJ ran the last thirty yards ahead of me, bouncing up to hug him and telling him about twelve things without taking a breath. "Oh, Standing Elk, I've missed you . . . been meaning to come see you for about two weeks . . . never understood why you won't let Daddy bulldoze a road in here . . . takes too long to walk . . . seems like I never can find time anymore."

He lowered those dried-up old eyes to her face, didn't smile—nothing obvious. But he was glad to see her. They went way back, those two. He nodded to her, pointed to a log by the fire. "Sit down."

He caught my eye and nodded toward the fire. For once, I was glad he was a mind reader. "You want rabbit?" A stick, spitted through a hunk of meat, was balanced between two forked ones over the fire. Rabbit. So that's what I was smelling. I'd never eaten it before but, man, it smelled great.

"You bet." I said, walking over to the other side of the fire to get away from the smoke. Then I remembered BJ. "How about you, Beej?"

"I'm not very hungry." She sat down on the log. The crows had finally shut up.

My fingers were numb, so I held them out over the fire till the feeling started coming back. Two crows flew back into the top of the trees. I looked closer at Standing Elk's face as he got the stick from across the fire. Pork must have been right: I didn't see any sign at all that he needed to shave.

He cut off a hunk of meat with his knife and handed it to me. The third crow dived down and landed in the dirt right at my feet. I jumped back, almost dropped the meat. That was one big bird. Its shiny black eyes were fixed on my meat, so I ate fast. I didn't exactly trust a bird that tame. It was so close I could see each feather, purple and green mixed into black like an oil slick. The rabbit tasted great, but the bird made me nervous. What would I do if it went for my meat? With those long toenails and that thick bill? I finished it in a hurry, licked the grease off my fingers, was ready for more.

But Standing Elk didn't offer more. For a minute, I thought he was going to. He cut another chunk off the rabbit before he put the stick back across the fire, but he dropped that piece on the ground by his own foot for the crow. It walked the way a wind-up toy does, stiff-legged, over to the meat; stabbed it with its beak; and then flew off down the river, the other two cawing after it. It was a relief when I couldn't hear them anymore. Things got on my nerves more at Standing Elk's.

BJ jumped up from the log then. "Standing Elk," she said, "I have something exciting to tell you. Rob and I are getting married." She stuck out her hand with the cigar ring.

Standing Elk didn't say a word, just stared at it like it wasn't great news. BJ's smile faded, and she lowered her hand back behind the purple mitten on her right hand.

Standing Elk wiped his knife blade on his jeans, pushed it into a holder on his belt, and eased himself down on a sitting log across from her. He started stirring the fire with a stick, like there was something important in there for him to see. The flame flared up, so maybe it *was* talking to him. Jesus, I remembered again why I hated coming here. You never knew what to expect. I noticed the rabbit hide hanging from a bush over behind the sitting log, blood still caked all over it.

Then, starting with a low rumble in his throat, Standing Elk spoke, but to me. His voice was so quiet and deep it took a minute to understand the few words said. "Best you do marry," he said. "Child needs a father."

Oh shit. He knew.

Then the crows came back, quiet this time, landed in the top of the tree over my head. Standing Elk twisted on his log to look at me.

I looked up at the crows, glad for an excuse not to face him. How much did he know, and what should I say? He waited till I got through watching them. For once, of course, when I wanted them to, they didn't raise hell at all.

I'd about decided to just come out and ask him how he knew when his head started nodding up and down—one, two, three times—like he was jump-starting himself to talk again. "Indian people," he finally said, "love all children. However, whenever born . . ." He sighed, his head nodding on, his sad face turned back to the fire. "White man . . . different."

He laid the stick down, reached into his shirt pocket, pulled out a packet of cigarette papers and a tobacco pouch. Poured some funny-looking tobacco out of the pouch into one paper and sealed it with his tongue. Picked the stick on the ground back up, stuck it in the fire, lit the cigarette, and took a long draw. Blew out the smoke, then fastened those black eyes back on me, his chin lifting, so I knew he was making sure I listened.

"Not a job for a boy." He drew on the cigarette, still staring right at me. "Important now, Robert. It is important you grow up fast. Become a brave man." A big breath, another draw. He set the cigarette down, held out both his bony hands, and shook hands with himself. "You and Roberta Jo," he said, "become one, strong together. There is much to face, much to face so young." A big sigh. "Be brave. Be a brave man . . ." His voice trailed off, and he picked up his cigarette, took a few draws on it, and looked back into the fire.

"Standing Elk." BJ's voice was small. She stood, took a step his way. "How long have you known about our baby?"

The sun went out then—just smack went out behind the clouds—and little hard pellets of snow, like bird shot, hissed into the fire and hammered us. The wind picked up, the next gust so hard it snuffed the fire into thick smoke and scattered the ashes.

Standing Elk raised his tired eyes to BJ, but he didn't answer her. Just kept staring like he was memorizing her face. Finally, he shook his head. Clear back in their slits, his eyes were shiny, maybe with tears. He looked unhappy; then, unhappier, he turned back to me.

"You take care of this good woman," he said. He ground out his cigarette in the red dirt by the fire and raised himself up from the log. "I go now." He walked past BJ to pick up the rabbit stick and shuffled off toward the two-room shack he'd built with boards he must have found. The hinges on his door creaked when he opened it and walked inside. He shut the door with a soft *ker-thud*. Never looked back, never answered BJ's question.

We both just stood there, emptiness hanging in the air; the crows too quiet above us; the fire smoke choking us; sharp, icy snow stinging our skin. And the door of the shack stayed shut. I reached for her hand and squeezed it because I couldn't think what the shit else to do.

Then I did for sure see tears—lots of them—streaming down BJ's face. "Rob," she said, "Standing Elk loves me like a daughter. He's blood, our relative—Daddy's half brother. He's never treated me like this. Why?"

"Maybe he just doesn't think he has a right to butt in, Beej." God, I hurt for her. How could that son of a bitch treat her like that? And how in the hell could he be Mr. Bonniface's brother? That was big news to me, but now wasn't the best time to ask her about that.

The wind was whipping the crows around in the top of the tree now. They flew down to a bush by the shack. I kept an eye on them and put my arms around Beej. Maybe a hug would help. Her warm body felt good against me. "We gotta get out of here, honey, or we'll freeze. This is turning into a real blizzard."

Tears were gushing down her face. "He has a perfect right to butt in. He's always helped when I've asked him to. My whole life! Standing Elk sees things other people don't, just like his mother did. He must know something he doesn't want me to know."

"BJ," I said through a lump in my throat, "goddamn him. I knew we shouldn't have come out here. There's got to be a logical reason he just talked to me and not you."

Her eyes were the palest blue I'd ever seen them, big and scared.

"Rob," she said in that husky little-girl voice, "what could Standing Elk know that he'd rather leave than tell me?"

chapter fifteen

We were lucky to make it back from Standing Elk's in one piece. The weather went all to hell, snow blowing so hard you couldn't see more than a foot ahead of you, stinging your hands and face. The log across the river had iced over. Even BJ said we couldn't cross. So we walked two or three miles back around the far side to the bridge, me turning into a frigging snowman in just my jean jacket. BJ got so weak and tired she could hardly pick up her feet the last half mile.

It took us ten minutes hunkered shivering over the truck heater to thaw out. BJ said I could get gas from her dad's tank at the barn, so at least I didn't have to worry about that. My hands burned when the feeling came back in them, and they didn't look their regular color. Each finger wiggled, though, so that was a good sign. BJ's cheeks were pinking up, too. "You look like a ghost coming back from the dead," I told her.

She crossed her arms like she had something on her mind. "I've decided that this may be the best time for us to tell Daddy. Mom left for High Rock this afternoon after your call, because Aunt Kitty's there. I think it'd be better to tell Daddy when Mom's not around."

I shrugged. "Your call, Beej." I didn't know what to expect, but my stomach knotted.

She didn't look as scared as I felt, heading up the walk to their big house. She opened their heavy front door and went in first. I stopped just a second, looked up at heaven, thinking maybe God would give me an idea about what to say. But no luck. All I saw was the sky looking as gray as an old navy blanket. So I took a breath like I was about to run a four-forty, rubbed the lucky buckeye in my pocket, stood up straight like Mom had always reminded me to, and walked through the Bonnifaces' door.

At least it was warm in there, out of the wind. Mr. Bonniface's twelve-gauge shotgun was hanging on a gun rack on the wall above me. A Remington pump, with a full box of shells on the table right under it. My hands got sweaty as I turned to their living room. The sound of my boots on the wood floor sounded like a prisoner walking to the gas chamber in a movie I saw once.

The fireplace in the living room crackled. Mr. Bonniface was in there; I knew that before I saw him, from the smell of his wet leather boots and cigarette smoke. No backing out now. My knees felt weak. I rubbed my buckeye between my sweaty fingers and walked on in.

The reading lamp by his chair was the only light. The rest of the room was shadowy. He looked up from his *Life* magazine with Vice President Nixon on the cover. Where the hell was BJ? Mr. Bonniface smiled at me, his feet propped up on his brown leather footstool. He had to special-order his cowboy boots because his feet were so big. Even sitting down, he looked huge.

"Oh, Rob, glad you're back. I was about to send out the Mounties. It's blowing up a doozy out there, isn't it?"

Before I could answer him, BJ came through the swinging door from the kitchen at the far end of the living room. She stepped down the one step into the room and smiled at me. "I put on some hot chocolate." She paused when she got to her dad and kissed him on the forehead. "We had to take the long way back from Standing Elk's, and we're both frozen solid."

The sky outside the window behind Mr. Bonniface was getting dark, even though it couldn't be later than four o'clock. Firelight bounced off the walls in a way that made the shadows too big, like the spook house at the carnival. It made the living room creepy. I looked down at the Indian symbols on the rug and tried to get a hold of myself. Took a couple more deep breaths, hoping what I should say would show up soon in my head. There was a bowl full of candy corn on the coffee table. I helped myself to a handful, but my mouth was so dry that I had trouble chewing. Mr. Bonniface was looking back and forth between BJ and me. He knew something was up.

"Daddy . . ." BJ's voice sounded little in the empty-feeling room. "Rob and I have something we want to talk to you about."

Well, there it was. I better jump in. "Wait, BJ." I walked across the room to her—a safe distance away from him— and tried to finish chewing the last of the candy. "I'll do the talking." I turned to Mr. Bonniface. "There is something that has happened, sir, which we want to tell you about." My voice bounced off the walls like those crazy shadows.

Mr. Bonniface put his magazine down on the end table, slid his feet off the footstool onto the floor, and frowned like he'd rather be reading. "Well, here I am." He folded both arms over his chest. "Shoot."

BJ took my hand. He noticed and frowned. We'd never held hands in front of him before. A log dropped in the fireplace, and sparks flared up. He kept staring at our hands. I swallowed the last of the candy. I was shaking now.

Mr. Bonniface pushed the footstool out of the way with one foot and stood up. He took a couple of steps toward us. "Well, out with it. What is it?" I hadn't remembered he was that much bigger than me, two or three inches taller and probably fifty pounds heavier.

"Well, sir . . ." It was hard to get my voice out. I shoved my free hand into my jean pocket for my buckeye. "We have come to find out, sir, that BJ is going to have a baby, Mr. Bonniface." I rubbed the buckeye, then kept going. "So we have decided to get married, and we hope you'll be happy about having a grandson . . . and all."

He wasn't happy. Even in the low light, I could see his face begin to turn red. I kept on talking. "I would be very happy to become a part of your family, Mr. Bonniface. I like your family very much, sir."

He still didn't move—just kept standing there, his cheeks getting redder and redder, a purple *Y*-shaped vein between his eyes standing out so far you could see his pulse pound in his forehead. Then, in one huge step, he was towering over me.

BJ let go of my hand and stepped away. Everything happened fast, but it felt like a slow-motion movie. All I could see anywhere was Mr. Bonniface filling up the whole room in front of me. Both his fists were clenched, and the sound of his breath was scary. He grabbed the collar of my jean jacket and lifted me up so high it about cut off the blood supply to my armpits. "You dumb little shit. Over my goddamned dead body you'll marry her." He stuck his nose up close to mine. "You're putting the dally before the lasso on this one, boy!"

I hoped he didn't remember the Remington. I wondered whether I should try to fight back or if that would make things worse, like it always had with my ole man?

"What *can* you two be thinking?" His face went an even darker purple red, a color I'd never seen on a living person before. I figured if he didn't murder me soon, he might rupture himself. "Let me get this straight!" he bellowed, letting go of my coat and dropping me hard, back to the floor. I caught my balance, stepped away from him. "BJ is pregnant! Pregnant! And if that's not bad enough, you two are going to make another mistake! Just like some goddamned follow-the-dot game, you have decided to get married. Well, the hell you will. The *hell*!"

I was so scared that I wanted to be dead, crawl under the rug, run for the truck—anything to get away from Mr. Bonniface. In my head, though, I remembered what Standing Elk had said: "Be a brave man . . . You take care of this good woman." I had to fight for us. I balled up my fists, feeling on the inside the same way I did the times my ole man had gone nuts.

Before I could talk, though, Mr. Bonniface started punching the air with his finger, jabbing it toward me each time he made a point. "What the hell are you two thinking? No daughter of mine will ever suck hind tit." He whirled and stomped over to the far side of the room. "Ever!" He pounded his fist against the paneled wall under a stuffed deer head. "Do you understand what I'm saying to you, boy?" He hit the wall again. Harder. "Do you? *Do you?*"

One of the deer's eyes came flying out of its head, landed at Mr. Bonniface's feet but didn't break. He kept yelling, stepped toward the eye, and kicked it so hard it bounced against the living room wall and went rattling out into the hall toward the front door. He folded his arms again, glared at me, his chest heaving like he'd run a kickoff return the length of a football field.

"No, sir," I said, feeling some safer with him there and me on the other side of the room. "I don't understand what you're saying, Mr. Bonniface." I couldn't believe how he was acting. He wasn't anything like the man I'd known for over two years. "I love BJ, Mr. Bonniface. Love her a lot. It was a bad mistake, but we can make it work. We can make it just fine. I've got a job, and we can live at my place for a while at first."

"God," he groaned, "turn on your headlights, boy. You're pissing in the wind. You want to make it 'just fine' like your papa and mama? Is that your idea of *fine*? Well, not with my daughter! You have a future, Rob." He kept pacing. "You're farting around with yours—and BJ's, too—if you both don't get an education. How in the hell could you two be so stupid?" He spun around at BJ, like a mammoth pissed-off buffalo, shaking its head before it charged. I took her hand back, moved closer to her, and gave it a squeeze.

Her face looked frostbitten. "Daddy, we were careful! We don't know why it happened." Her voice wobbled. "But what else can we do?" I put my arm around her shoulders. Little as BJ was, he must have looked terrifying to her. Mr. Bonniface's eyes narrowed. I had to protect her. I could tell she was trying hard not to cry, her eyes looking big and scared. A tear dribbled down her cheek. Hell, I wanted to cry for her.

"Well, there won't be any marriage," he said, "because I won't let there be. She's underage, and I won't sign." His face had started fading back to a better color. BJ's tear must have got to him.

I found my courage again. "Sir, this is a confused situation. If we don't get married, what else *can* we do? I mean, I'm not trying to be stupid, Mr. Bonniface, but I want to do right by her. If you have any other ideas . . ."

He nodded like he had at least heard me and turned back to the fireplace. He walked across to the hearth, picked up a log, and threw it on the fire, then kicked it hard to the back of the andirons before he threw on another one and sparks flew.

She turned to me and rolled her eyes. I wiped the tear off her cheek with my thumb.

After he'd poked the fire a couple more times with the heel of his boot, he went back to his brown leather chair and dropped into it like a heavy feed sack. He stretched out his legs and glared at the toes of his big boots for a long time.

My head was dizzy. My stomach wanted to barf, but at least I was alive. I figured I better just stand there, keep my mouth shut, and wait. I squeezed BJ's shoulder every now and then to let her know I understood and listened to the tick-ticktock of the big grandfather clock in the hall.

Finally, when I didn't think I could stand the pressure anymore, his eyes came to my face, and he shook his head. "No shit," he said. "This is indeed one confused situation. I trusted you to do better by her than this. I want some time to think. In the meantime, I don't want either of you to talk to anyone else—particularly your mother, BJ. Who else knows about this?"

"Just Doc Justice, Daddy. No one else." BJ was breathing a little easier, too. I could tell by her voice.

And Standing Elk, I thought. *He knows it, too.* I didn't say it, though.

"Well, at least you've exercised *some* judgment." He nodded and tried to smile, but his upper lip curled the way a dog's does when it snarls at a stranger. He pulled a pack of Luckies out of his shirt pocket, tapped out one, and lit it. His hands shook when he struck a match, which lit up his face. That vein in his forehead was still standing out up there. After he took a couple of drags, his face got to looking almost normal. "You get the hell out of here, Rob. I need time to cool down. BJ and I have a lot to talk about. It's a piss-poor situation, but we'll sort it out."

"Mr. Bonniface," I said, "I don't want to leave. I want to be in on the deciding. I have a responsibility here for what's happened."

"Well, well, well." He took another long drag on his Lucky. "Mr. Responsibility. You're a little late for that now, boy."

"Wait, Daddy!" BJ's voice was stronger. "I *want* Rob here."

His eyebrows raised, but his voice came out controlled and reasonable. "BJ, God only knows Rob helped create this problem, but right now, I don't see that there's much he can do to solve it." He ground the half-smoked cigarette out in a green ashtray by his chair, stood up again, walked over to us, and put his arm around her shoulders on top of mine. I had to move away to be polite. "We've never found anything

111

yet we couldn't lick—have we, honey?" He smiled down at her, then gave me a look over the top of her head that said *Two's company and three's a crowd.*

Her eyelashes were blinking too fast. She was fighting back tears again when she looked up from under his arm. We both knew I had to go. "Okay," she said. "I'll walk Rob to the door."

I tried to smile at him as I turned to follow her. "I'll be seeing you, Mr. Bonniface."

He nodded but didn't answer. I kicked the deer eye in the hall. It rolled over to the front door and slammed against it. BJ reached down, scooped up the eye, and dropped it into the pocket of that yellow coat.

From where he was standing in the living room, I knew he could see us. But I didn't care. I pulled her up to me, buried her in my arms, and hugged her as long and as close as I wanted to. The hell with him. The smell of her hair, how silky it was against my nose, softened the fear in my heart. "Beej," I whispered so he couldn't hear, "don't leave me out. There's only one thing you can do about babies besides having them. You don't have to do that. Don't let him talk you—"

"BJ." He'd stepped into the living room end of the hall, glaring at us. "The hot chocolate is burning. I can smell it clear in here. Tell him goodbye. You'll have plenty of time to talk to Rob tomorrow."

I reached for the doorknob. "Promise?" I begged her. "Promise you won't do anything without talking to me."

She nodded, gave me a *Please go* look, and rolled her eyes back over her shoulder at her dad.

"I'll call tonight." I opened the door and stepped out.

The temperature had dropped even more. A mean blast of winter air took away my breath. I waved to her out the truck window as I headed for the barn. When I hit that loose cattle guard in the turn, my wheels shimmied so bad it took both hands to steer the truck. I looked back in my rearview mirror to wave again, but she was gone.

chapter sixteen

I didn't cut the radio on the whole way home, just drove along in the snow-made quiet, trying to sort out what had happened. It felt like Alaska in the cab of the truck; even my good heater wouldn't warm it up. About a mile after the Bonnifaces' gate, I swerved to miss something black on the road. About the size of a dead crow. Maybe the greedy one that ate the rabbit. Once I got by it, though, I saw it was just a piece of tire retread.

Boy, I felt rotten, wished I could retread myself, cover all the crap I'd gotten into with something new and good. I moved the shoulder Pork had slugged; it didn't feel all that great, either. Retread my whole frigging life—that's what I wanted to do. Everything I'd said to Mr. Bonniface today seemed wrong. What else could I have done? Shit, maybe I was just hungover.

Snow was starting to drift, white and lumpy like giant marshmallows up on the hills, brown and splotched along the road where cars threw up dirt. Toasted marshmallows. Nothing I thought of cheered me up. I wasn't even hungry.

The wind whistled around the cab in the open country beyond the canyon. Not much of anybody on the road. A Jeep passed me on the edge of town. I didn't even hear it coming. It was like wearing earmuffs when that much snow piled up. I tried singing to clear my head and re-membered an old Pecos Bill song from when I was a kid. *Yippee-i-ay-i-ya, yippee-i-o. He's the toughest critter west of the Alamo.* Over and over, all the way home, I kept singing it, and it helped at little.

Our little white house looked real good to me when I pulled in at five o'clock. I went in and yelled for Mom, was hoping she'd be there, even though I planned on keeping the secret like I had promised. Nobody answered. The house was as cold as the freezer room at Safeway. She'd left me a note on the table. *Over at Rose and Carl's. Come eat with us if you get home before six. Love, Mom.*

Well, bag that. Even though I was hungry, I was in no mood to deal with Carl Jr. So I stoked the furnace in the basement, came upstairs, and made a bowl of chicken noo-dle soup and three peanut butter and banana sandwiches. Poured two glasses of milk and sat down at the kitchen table to study my playbook. Homecoming was next weekend, the scout coming from UW. Coach wanted to try out a couple of new pass patterns, but the *x*'s and *o*'s started running together. I was crying like a baby. The way Mr. Bonniface had treated me must have been more than I could take. My brain had also gone fuzzy again. I just couldn't think up what to do next, since Mr. Bonniface had taken over BJ and canceled all my getting-married plans.

I turned on the radio to get my mind off my troubles, but that didn't help, either. It was too snowy to go outside, so I went up to my room, lay down on the bed, and ended up bawling some more. Standing Elk wouldn't think I was much of a man, but what else could I do? I wished I'd asked BJ about him being related to Mr. Bonniface. She may have told me some family secret I wasn't supposed to know, because she'd never said anything about that before.

At seven thirty, I called BJ and got Mrs. Bonniface. "She's down at the barn with her daddy, Rob. That little bay mare Don got her last Christmas got tangled in some barbed wire. They're sewing her up. Funny, though . . ." Her voice got dimmer, like she'd turned away from the phone. "They left the sulfa powder here on the counter." Then louder again. "They probably have more down in the barn. This is quite a blizzard, isn't it? Did you have any trouble getting home?"

"Not really. The roads weren't that bad. It was just a little hard to see. Mrs. Bonniface, I really need to talk to BJ when she comes in. It's important."

"Sure thing," she said. "Oh, Rob, by the way—what went on over here this afternoon? Were you all playing polo in the living room?" She laughed. "The lamp shades are crooked, and something knocked the eye out of that deer head on the wall. It's completely missing. Do you have any idea where it could be?"

My heart squeezed in my chest. I was having trouble paying attention to what she was saying. I *had* to talk to BJ. "No, Mrs. Bonniface, I don't have any idea. You will have her call me, won't you? The minute she gets in?"

"Sure will. Take care, now."

Maybe I was still hungry. I emptied a half box of Wheaties in a bowl, finished them off, and went back to lying on my bed. Took out a knife and cleaned my fingernails. I remembered when I got to my right thumb where BJ had put the deer eye: in the pocket of that yellow coat. I'd remind her to tell her mom when she called me back. I tried picturing in my head how BJ looked on the inside now with our baby growing in her. All different in there, but nothing different on the outside except maybe that little pooch. Funny, the way your body can hide secrets from you. I remembered the time my jaw had started aching and how surprised I was when that wisdom tooth came boring through.

I finally fell asleep, didn't wake up till the next day, Sunday, my pillow still damp against my cheek. Mom had covered me up and left me to sleep in my clothes.

"No," she said, stirring the breakfast oatmeal when I asked about BJ. "She didn't call last night. I got back about nine o'clock and didn't leave again."

On Monday morning, at school, I hung out around BJ's locker till the first-period bell rang. No BJ. No Beej second period or even after third. So when everyone else headed to the cafeteria for lunch, I went back to her locker to check once more. It was like swimming up a river full of Alaskan salmon the wrong way. Locker doors banging; people pushing each other, yelling.

I saw Nella's red ponytail coming toward me. Her face lit up when she saw me. Great. She wanted to talk.

"Hi, Rob. Where's BJ? I've been looking for her all day." Nella, speed-talking. "She's not sick again, is she? Is she sick again? Because she wasn't out front this morning or in homeroom or English, either."

"Jesus, Nella!" I yelled over the noise. "Figure it out yourself. It doesn't take a genius. She's not here! I can't keep up with where BJ is every minute of the day."

Her smile went flat as a tire, and she got this hurt look. "Well, *excuse* me for bothering you. Somehow, for some unknown reason, I thought you might care."

Girls pick the damnedest times to get all sensitive. I just let it go, shrugged my sore shoulder as she pushed past me and went twitching away down the hall. Then relief flooded me like a cold shower after a workout because Beej was at her locker. I ran to meet her.

"God, BJ." I couldn't get my arms around her fast enough. "Why didn't you call last night? Where have you been all morning?"

She pulled away from my hug, looking surprised I was upset.

"I've been nuts. *Nuts!*" I said. "You never called me back. What happened after I left?"

"Calm down. Take a breath. One question at a time." Her eyes were the exact swirly colors of a blue-agate shooter I'd had in the third grade. She reached for my hand, her fingers still cold. So she must have just come in from outside. She peeked over my shoulder at Blotnick's door, then kissed me and smiled. I was confused about what was making her so happy.

"After you left," she said, "Daddy was great. We turned on the space heater in Domino's old stall in the barn and finished talking. He told Mom we were sewing up Belle, so she didn't suspect a thing. It took a while. He asked me about a million questions, so it was too late to call when we came back to the house. I didn't want to wake your mom." She stooped down to look at herself in a mirror she kept glued inside her locker door. "Daddy just listed all the possibilities and talked to me about them." She stopped to put on some lipstick, blotted her lips together, smiled at herself in the mirror, and put her lipstick back in her purse. I noticed the cigar ring was missing.

"Is he still pissed?" I asked her. "Or did your dad finally see us getting married was the right thing?"

She smiled again—a quick smile that came and went like the marriage idea went out of style yesterday. I was thinking how much better BJ was looking. The purple smudges under her eyes were almost gone. Her dad must have found some miracle pill. I wondered if he'd made her take off the ring or if she'd done it on her own. How much would a real ring cost?

"We spent an hour with Doc Justice this morning, just Daddy and me." She slammed her locker closed and wiggled the handle. "That's where I've been." There wasn't anybody left in the hall, but she talked quiet, the way you do in a waiting room. She turned to go to the lunchroom, still talking. "Doc wasn't any more help. He told Daddy the exact same things he'd told me. That there was nothing legal he could do; plus, it would be really hard on me to have an abortion as far along as I was."

She had on the kind of sleeveless dress that goes over a sweater. It stuck real tight to her body down to her waist. Bright pink, and a white sweater under it. My class ring, on a gold chain hanging round her neck, was buried somewhere down between her breasts. They were definitely growing like Rose's had.

"Are you listening to me, Rob? You look funny."

"Sorry," I told her. "My mind got distracted by the way that dress fits you."

"Dress? What dress?" She looked down and laughed. "This isn't a dress. It's a jumper. Where was I? This is important. Oh yeah. Doc said if there was anybody he'd do it for—an abortion—it would be us, but the state could jerk his license. He just couldn't risk it."

Good, I was thinking. *At least Doc's talking sense.* "So was Doc for us getting married?" We turned the corner and headed down a long hall, the smell of the food in the lunchroom at the far end making me hungry.

"Actually, he wasn't, but he was proud of you for offering." BJ lowered her voice; we were passing a study hall now. I still couldn't figure out why BJ was looking so relieved. "Daddy and Doc just discussed options. *Options* was Daddy's word. 'You only have one good option at your age,' Doc told us. 'That's the home for unwed mothers in Denver.' I could pretend I was going to Europe next semester, some story like that, and just stay there till the baby's born and give it up for adoption."

"Why in the hell would you do that?"

"Not so loud, Rob. Someone in study hall might hear us. Let me finish. No one in Juniper would ever have to know. All kinds of people who can't have their own kids would love to have our baby. Doc knows a doctor who can line it all up." BJ was talking fast, like she was talking herself into the idea.

I stopped in front of the water fountain and stared at her. "BJ, what in the hell are you thinking? You wouldn't *really* go for that, would you? I'll bet your dad wouldn't, either. He wouldn't want other people getting their hands on *his* grandson."

She nodded her head. "You're right about that, grandson or granddaughter. He didn't like the adoption idea. Said someone always finds out, and pretty soon, everyone in Juniper would know anyway." She lowered her voice to sound like her father's. "'Your grandmother Marion would turn over in her grave. We have our family's reputation to think of. No decent man would have you once it was out.'"

So where did that leave me? Undecent?

BJ tucked her arm in mine and moved up closer. "But it's not going to come down to that, because Daddy has a better solution." Today, she smelled like Jergens Lotion. "I'm just not ready to get married, Rob. Daddy's right: we're too young. It would cut off *our* options. You couldn't play ball in college. I wouldn't get to go to Wellesley and then to vet school. You know, we'd have to give up our dreams."

Walking next to BJ was hard. She wandered off her line—crooked, back and forth—like a beginning bike rider. She bumped into me and laughed at herself. "Daddy thought me writing Trina Gumpert about the abortion deal was a good start." She bumped me again, smiled but kept walking. "Even though Doc really disagreed."

She slowed down to look at herself in the glass top of a door, ran her fingers through her hair. We were alone in the hall. "Doc says we have to find somebody fast, and there aren't many good people who do this kind of thing safely." She smiled. "But Daddy says they're out there, and he'll find them. He's dead set against us getting married, Rob. Says he won't sign for permission, and we will find the right person, and I'll be okay." She ran her fingers through her bangs. "Is that piece of hair still sticking up on my head?"

"BJ! Christ!" I grabbed her by both shoulders and made her look at me. "To hell with your hair. To hell with your dad. Listen to Doc. Abortions are dangerous! You don't know what could happen." She was scaring the shit out of me.

She put her finger up to her lips and sighed like I was missing her point. "Don't get all serious on me now, Robert

Eric Hitchcock. Remember, you're the one whose precious Bohingi Boys were more important than talking about this only four short days ago."

I grabbed her arm, really pissed off, but she laughed. She'd been teasing me. So I let go of her.

"Daddy loves me better than anything in the world. He's just trying to figure out what's best for you and me."

My head felt stuffed with cotton. My throat hurt. I couldn't think of what else to say. I had to talk her out of this. Inside me, just a little bit, the idea of not having to get married did feel a little good—college ball, fraternities, freedom. But it seemed too easy. "It's not the right thing, Beej. I'm sure of it. It's not the way we should be thinking."

We were at the open double doors of the cafeteria, and the food smells made my stomach growl. From the far side of the room—naturally—Nella spotted us, stood up and starting waving like a spastic wide receiver. There were too many people around to talk anymore now. Chairs scraping, people yelling. Somebody threw a roll, and it bounced off the table in front of us. Jimmy Simons, the only freshman on the varsity football team, was looking my way, wearing his hero-worship face.

Of course Nella made it across the room in record time, grabbed BJ's arm, looked at me like I was a douchebag, and started firing a bunch of dumb questions about the homecoming skit. "Angie only has three blonde wigs. Do you have time to go down to Stevens Fryberger and see if they'll loan us two more?" BJ gave me an *I'm sorry* look and followed Nella, who was still talking.

I headed for Jimmy's table. His face lit up like a Christmas tree when I set my books down by him and sat down. I had to talk BJ out of this.

+ + +

The rest of the week was crazy, Coach keeping us late every day at practice. I had to focus on the homecoming game Friday night. If we beat Casper, we'd be state champs. My arm was still a little stiff where Pork had slugged me, but the hurt was working itself out. Coach looked disgusted when he noticed the bruise. "Bohingi Boys' initiation, I presume?"

Mr. Delaney, the scout from UW, came Thursday afternoon to watch me. I had a good practice. When I came out of the shower afterward, I passed Coach's office slow enough to hear him bragging on me. "He's one quality football player, Ed. A good-character kid who hasn't begun to realize his potential. He runs the forty in five-three and has great foot speed. He has the makings of a fine college back."

I got all swelled up, couldn't hardly wait till I got home to call Beej, but when I got her, she sounded upset. "I just got off the phone with Trina Gumpert. She was no help at all. Says she's a Catholic and wouldn't help me find someone who did abortions even if she could. You know what she said, Rob?" BJ's voice went high and pissed. "'Anyone who doesn't have the strength of character to wait deserves to pay the price.' Can you believe it? And I really liked her when she lived here."

"Aw, don't let her get to you, Beej. People change." I wished I could get a word in to tell her about Mr. Delaney.

"Well, it does worry me because Daddy hasn't found anybody else. But then"—her voice cheered up—"he's just started working on it. Really, I'm sure he will. Oh brother . . ." BJ's voice went trailing off. "Here comes Mom's car. I'll talk to you later. I was supposed to have all this chicken fried. Maria's taken the day off, and I've been asleep on the couch since I got home."

"Okay," I said. "Suit yourself. I guess you got no interest in knowing who it was just got elected to the homecoming court."

"What? Wait! I do, too!" I heard a sizzle. She must have dropped the chicken in some fat. "How do you know? I thought it was all supposed to be a secret till tomorrow. Tell me."

"Naw," I said. "Coach told me, but you're too busy frying chicken."

"Robert Eric Hitchcock, that's not fair. I have time to hear *that*. Hurry up. Mom's opening the car door. She's getting out."

"You're right, BJ. It should be a secret." I loved teasing her. "Don't know what came over me, why I even brought it up."

"Rob!" She screamed so loud I pulled the phone away from my ear. "I can't wait till tomorrow. Tell me. The smell of this chicken's making me sick, anyway. Hang on. I'll tell Mom I don't feel good and get on the other phone so we can talk."

"Nope," I said. "I gotta go meet Pork in the park, throw a little ball to loosen up my arm."

"Rob, wait, wait!" She was yelling in the phone when I hung up, laughing. Went to get my football and headed out the door, humming "Have Gun Will Travel." Paladin—now there was a real man. Actually, he reminded me of Pork in a way.

I knew I'd have to get serious about talking her out of this abortion idea after homecoming. But for now, Coach was about to call her with some news that would cheer her up for sure.

chapter seventeen

The kitchen clock over the sink said seven o'clock when I got home from Kendrick Park. Mom had a box of starch in one hand and the phone in the other. She smiled, handed me the phone, and started pouring starch into the washing machine. I knew it would be Beej because Coach had said he'd call right after practice to give her plenty of time to get her clothes ready for tomorrow.

"So, Mr. Smarty Pants," her chirpy little voice was saying, "I didn't need your help, after all. I found out right after you hung up who the homecoming queen is." Then she sounded formal. "Mr. Hitchcock, would you be my escort for the homecoming court presentation sixth period tomorrow, and again at halftime in the Casper game? That is, assuming you plan to be there." I was real happy for her. She deserved some good news for a change. Her voice turned fake mad. "You're such a stinker for not telling me all about it this afternoon. I ought to ask somebody else."

"Yeah, but you won't." I untangled the phone cord from the kitchen-table leg and headed for the living room. Mom frowned, pointed at the beans on the stove. She'd be pissed if I didn't hang up and eat when dinner was ready.

I nodded, waved her off for a minute, and stretched the cord as far as it would go into the living room. "You wouldn't ask anybody else, Beej, because the queen needs the king." I lay down on the sofa. Mom followed me, motioned for me to get my feet off it. So I pulled off both shoes, stretched out my legs, and wiggled my toes. I wished Mom would disappear back into the kitchen, and—like a miracle—she did. Dishes and silverware started banging around in there. "The way I'm going to throw that football tomorrow night, BJ Bonniface, you wouldn't want anybody else for your king."

BJ started filling me in on a bunch of stuff I pretty much knew: what I'd have to wear (coat and tie—puke), when to show up . . . all girl shit. I sort of paid attention because I knew it was important to her, but my mind was wandering to Tom Toliver, Casper's big center. The only way I wouldn't get smeared by him was my quick release. He'd knocked the wind out of me last year. At least I was throwing good, my arm loosened up just fine. I'd hit Pork dead-on three times halfway across Kendrick Park and nailed all but two of the little down-and-out patterns he ran for me. I liked the way I felt about twenty-four hours before a big game, my blood pounding stronger in my veins. Gave me the feeling I could do anything.

"Rob?"

"Huh?"

"You didn't answer. Are you listening? Be at the back gym door right at the end of fifth period, okay?"

"Yes, ma'am. Yes, Miss Homecoming Queen. I got it, but I'll see you in the morning before that." Mom came to the kitchen door and gave me her your-dinner-is-ready frown. Pointed at the macaroni and cheese and the beans on the kitchen table. "Beej, I'm real happy for you. You'll be the prettiest homecoming queen they ever had, and I'll be proud to be there with you, but I got to go now. Mom's waiting dinner on me."

"Well, okay." She sounded disappointed. It seemed like I had a natural knack for pissing off all women. "But I really do need to talk to you when you've got more time." Her voice went from talk to whisper. "Daddy called from Casper, Rob. Mom thinks he's at the stockyards, looking at a bull, but he stayed over because he got the name of a woman to do the baby deal. He's going to try and get me an appointment with her next week."

Talk about a crappy situation: Mom there, tapping her foot while BJ announces the abortion like it's a done deal. Not to mention I needed to keep my mental focus on Casper. "Christ!" I must have yelled into the phone, because Mom looked up, surprised. "Christ, BJ, you can't do that! We *got* to talk. Okay? *Got* to talk! I'll call you right after dinner."

And I tried, too, for two frigging hours, after I'd finally gotten through dinner with Mom, who was pissed at me for taking the Lord's name in vain again and excited about BJ being the homecoming queen. I had to act like I cared when I needed to be finishing that late Shakespeare paper, going over pass patterns, and definitely calling BJ. Her line stayed busy till eleven, when I gave up. Sometimes Mrs. Bonniface and her sister got to assing around on the phone, and it went on forever. I had to hit the rack. Too much was riding on tomorrow.

+ + +

Friday was a great football day, cold and clear, the sky the color of a pair of jeans when you get them faded just right.

The kind of day that just makes you want to run because of how great the wind feels against your skin. I decided I'd forget my problems and concentrate on nothing—nothing all day but winning that game.

Pork gave me a cheesy smile when I came by his locker that morning, grabbed my shirt from behind, and boxed a couple of body blows into my kidneys like he was making sure I was still tough. "You ready to smear them, Baby Cakes? We're counting on that arm tonight." He had on a new baseball hat. It was yellow, with PERVERT written in big black ballpoint pen letters across the front.

"Nice hat," I told him. "What I need is a big pervert between me and Toliver tonight. You buy me the time, I'll deliver the goods."

"Done." He laughed. "Don't know if it's just a good story, but I saw Coach in the parking lot this morning. He says there's a rumor that Toliver has a groin pull and may not play tonight." Pork smiled like a pervert. "Do you know how much damage I could do to that little fairy, Ralphie Smith, Casper plays behind him?" He threw back his head and laughed.

"Fuck, man," I said, "I could deal with dodging Ralphie instead of goddamned Tank Toliver any day." I gave Pork a goodbye slug. "I'm counting on you tonight, Pervert. I gotta go find my woman."

He laughed, stripped off his hat, and threw it in his locker. Pork would be history if Mr. Gagney saw him in that hat. Amazing how Pork stayed right on the edge of trouble. The bang of his locker door made me jump. Pregame jitters, Coach would say.

When I finally spotted BJ coming down the hall just before classes started, her skin was the greenish color of the locker behind her. "Jesus, Beej, what's wrong? I tried to call you all night. Shit, you look awful." I put my arm around her and steered her to a quiet place under the stairs, where we could talk.

"Thanks for the vote of confidence," she said, then shook her head like she was sorry she'd talked that way. "It's okay about last night. Aunt Kitty again. She and Mom talked half the night." BJ sighed. "I feel rotten. I've started throwing up at the dumbest times. Things smell different than they're supposed to. Like coffee, Rob. Coffee! I go in the kitchen in the morning, and the first smell of it makes me nauseous. Mom, of course, thinks I can't leave home without a good breakfast." BJ threw both her hands in the air. "So I start every day losing my cookies. Mom thinks it's because I've exhausted myself. Says either I go to bed for the whole weekend or she's personally taking me in to Doc Justice for a mono test. She only let me come today because of"—BJ whispered—"the homecoming deal. Right now, I don't even care about that. I wish I could just curl up in bed and sleep forever. Maybe I have mono, besides this." She gave her belly a disgusted look and sighed even bigger. "Plus, Daddy couldn't find the Casper woman. He called to tell me this morning." Her voice was a sad whisper. "She's disappeared—the woman has. Nobody in town knows where she's gone. He's completely struck out."

That was good news to me, but I didn't act like it. At least I didn't have to worry about talking her out of an abortion today.

"Daddy's got some other idea." She chewed on the edge of her lip. She had on a green sweater that showed off her tits and covered up the little tummy she was getting. I wanted to drag her farther back under the stairs, hold her tight, and make her feel better. We'd been apart from each other that way for too damn long.

Her eyes were pink-rimmed, a funny flat-blue color. "Rob, do you think this is all normal? Doc didn't say I'd feel this bad."

"Jesus, Beej, I don't know. Rose is all I know about it. I don't think she was throwing up all the time." I was worried, too. She looked so damn little. I got to wondering if she'd be able to take all the weight and pain of having my kid. I didn't want BJ to suffer because of me.

Her eyes got full of tears. "Rob, I'm afraid all of a sudden."

I dropped my notebook and put my arms around her. The hell with Blotnick, the hell with Miss Cantor, the hell with all of them. Nobody much came back this way, anyhow. I held her as close as I could. We stood there, hanging on to each other for the longest time. I kissed the top of her head. Smelling her clean smell always relaxed something inside me. Well, relaxed until I looked up and saw Nella about a foot away from BJ, peeking under the staircase with her arms folded across her chest. Instead of the usual goofy Nella grin, she had on a disgusted look.

"What ails *you*?" I asked her over BJ's shoulder. "Are we breaking some Nella commandment?"

"No," she said in a snotty little know-it-all voice. "I thought I might find you here. Not *my* commandment, but"—she tossed her ponytail like she was head of the manners patrol—"don't let me rush you or anything. I'd be interested in knowing, when BJ sees fit, just exactly what we're supposed to do with these wigs for the homecoming skit. The three of us have been waiting out front, right where she told us to meet her at eight fifteen, but she obviously has more important things to do!" Another toss of her ponytail.

BJ jerked out of my arms. "Oh, Nella, I'm so sorry! I forgot all about it." She gave me a helpless look, grabbed her books, and followed Nella back down the hall. Just as she made the turn to the front door, the class bell rang, and I jumped again. Worst case of pregame jitters I ever had.

Coach got the whole football team excused to eat lunch in the locker room together, so I didn't see BJ again till two thirty, when I met her in the hall outside the gym door. I was praying my sport coat wouldn't rip right down the back. I hadn't worn it since last spring, when Carl gave me his old one. Hard to believe I'd grown out of it already. I pulled my shoulders together to get as much slack as I could across the back, could feel the material strain every time I relaxed them. Had to keep my shirtsleeves pulled down, too, so you couldn't tell the coat sleeves were too short.

Lorna Casey and Midge were the other two girls on the court. Nella had come in fourth, missed it by two votes. I'd voted for her myself, but she'd been such a shit lately, I was half-glad she lost. Lorna and Midge were sticking close to BJ in the drafty hall outside the gym door, whispering and looking embarrassed and goose-pimply in strapless dresses. What is it about girls? You can have a whole big hallway with room to throw a ball and stretch, but you put a couple of girls in it, and they clump together like Scottie magnets. Seemed like BJ was always buried under friends when I needed to talk to her.

We had to wait quite a while in the hall, the cheerleaders screaming out "Beat Casper!" cheers, then Nella taking BJ's place narrating the skit. The skit must have been funny. You could hear people laughing. But I just kept looking at Beej. She had on the long light-pink dress she'd worn to prom. It had fit pretty tight on the top last spring, with just two little strings over her shoulders to hold it up. Now it was barely holding together, stretched skin-tight over her tits and her sides. Her dress and my sport coat—both too little but for real different reasons. God, she made my mouth water. The skirt on her dress had layers of that stiff see-through material they make ballet dancers' skirts out of, and it stood out so far you couldn't see her pooch at all. She had my class ring on a chain around her neck but was still missing the cigar ring on her finger. I kept meaning to ask her about that.

When Lorna and Midge finally left BJ alone to put their ears to the gym doors and listen to the skit, I leaned over to her. "You look awful pretty," I whispered. "You're feeling better, aren't you?"

She looked up at me and smiled. "I do feel better. I kept down some lunch. But"—she crossed her fingers so I could see them—"this dress is too tight. I'm praying it doesn't tear."

"I noticed." I licked my lips.

Rusty Barclay, Lorna's escort, showed up next. He cracked the door of the gym so we could all hear what was going on, then draped both arms over Lorna's shoulders. BJ looked at Rusty's back and rolled her eyes. Nella would really be pissed when her steady showed up out there, escorting Lorna, and I couldn't blame her. But it didn't surprise me. It just proved that Rusty, the big senior-class president, was a gen-u-ine phony, the kind of guy who thinks his shit can't stink, always looking out for number one. I never did understand how Nella could like a guy who examined his own earwax under a microscope for fun.

The Pep Band had started playing the song they play for graduations, "Pomp and . . ." something that never made any sense. First, Mr. Gagney—old Gag-a-Knee— announced Lorna and Rusty over the loudspeaker, and they went through the door into the gym. Midge and Ted Lackman came next. Midge had asked Ted since Mike was down at the university. "Ladies and gentlemen, may I have your attention, have your attention . . ." Gagney was getting the crowd ready for us.

I straightened my back, pulled my shoulders together. So far, the coat was holding. Then Gagney said, "It gives me great pleasure to introduce to you Juniper High's 1959 homecoming queen, Miss Roberta Jo Bonniface, and her escort, Mr. Robert Eric Hitchcock."

We stepped into the gym, and I had to blink. All the drums in the band must have been rolling at once, and there was a bright spotlight in our eyes. Everybody started clapping and cheering. BJ squeezed my arm. When we got to the middle of the floor, I looked down and gave her my proudest smile. It felt good to see her smiling back so big. My coat made a little tearing sound just as Miss Cantor put the diamond-looking crown on BJ's head. The crown slid off sideways. The band had stopped playing, and everybody laughed. I straightened up more, hoping they were laughing at the slippery crown and not my coat. Miss Cantor was a be-prepared kind of guidance counselor. She reached in her dress pocket, came out with a handful of bobby pins, and handed them to BJ. Both of them worked together till they got the crown stuck on pretty straight.

"Congratulations, BJ," she said to Beej. "We've never had a nicer queen." Then Miss Cantor pointed to the outside door. The Pep Band struck up the Juniper fight song, and we led the way out to the parking lot, where the parade was supposed to begin. I jerked my coat off the minute we got out the door, was relieved there was no tear on the outside, only the lining. Then I steered BJ over to the parking lot through a battalion of congratulating girls.

BJ, riding in a blue Buick convertible from Nella's dad's dealership, was supposed to be the last thing in the home-coming parade. The band, a car full of cheerleaders, three BEAT CASPER floats, and Lorna and Midge in another convertible all would go ahead of her. I was helping her stuff the skirt of her dress into the back seat of the Buick when her eyes got big. "I'm going to be sick," she whispered. "What should I do?"

Before I could think of an answer, Nella and about three thousand more screaming girls surrounded the car. "Stand back and give her a little air," I told Nella. "She's not feeling the greatest."

Nella gave me a mean look. "You're the only one that can get near without making her sick, I see. In case you don't remember, she was my friend long before you ever even knew her, Rob Hitchcock!"

"Get lost, Nella." She was probably extra pissed because of Rusty. I turned back to Beej. "Try to breathe real deep," I told her. "That helps me when I get creamed on a tackle."

About ten million blue-and-yellow crepe paper banners were draped all over the car. One on the antenna snapped me in the face. Nella laughed and walked away. Beej was breathing deep and trying to smile at all the people gathered around, congratulating her. The band began the fight song again, and people yelled, "Beat Casper! Beat Casper!" at the end of every verse. It was getting cold. BJ shivered. I would, too, if my shoulders were sticking out in the wind that way. Not that I'd ever wear a girl's dress or anything.

Then, Jesus! Out of nowhere, Nella reappeared, and she was bringing BJ a *cup of coffee*. "Remember the Thomas Dewey Parade?" she screamed, pushing her way through the crowd. "Drinking hot chocolate up by the war memorial to keep warm? At least you had a snowsuit then! See if this doesn't warm you up. I got it in the lunchroom."

I dived for the coffee too late. Nella jerked it away and spilled about half a cup all over BJ's lap. And it was seeping down through all the little holes and layers of the dress. BJ's eyes got huge and scared. Thanks to Nella, she was now *wearing* coffee. BJ gagged, fought down another gag, took a desperate deep breath.

What could I do? The wind picked up enough to tear one of the streamers off the antenna. Danny Owensby, who was driving for Nella's dad, climbed in, started the car, and pulled away from the curb. I remembered my sport coat, ran along the side of the car, and threw it onto the back seat. Maybe she could smother the smell with my coat. She grabbed it, her eyes saying *Thank you*, and put it over her lap as they rounded the corner and headed down the hill to Main Street.

When they were almost out of sight, I remembered to yell to her, "I'll wait for you at the Wyo! Meet me there when it's over." She nodded, looking relieved, so I knew she'd heard me.

Then I pushed my way through all the congratulating people, doing my damnedest to ignore Nella, who was screaming at me like somebody out of a bad dream. "Why can't I even do *one* thing nice for her? You just have to have her all to yourself, don't you? You're some kind of a selfish . . . selfish bastard!"

Jesus, *bastard* from Nella was strong language. But I couldn't explain, so I just kept going, headed for the parking lot to get to the pickup and beat the crowd downtown. BJ'd have to get home and rest up before the dance, and I had an important game to think about.

Coach must have seen me leaving. He yelled across the parking lot, "Rob, hold up! *The Casper Gazette* has a note on Toliver, something about a muscle pull in practice yesterday. There's a chance he won't be able to play tonight." Coach caught up with me, put his arm around my shoulder. "We need to take a look at adjusting our offense down the middle. If Casper plays Smith at center, Ramseur will eat his lunch. Come on in my office for a minute, will you?"

He turned to the gym, and I followed him, really worried about getting to BJ. I noticed how big his shoulders looked in his brown tweed sport coat—plenty of shoulder room in that coat—how confident he walked. I followed him into the locker room and prayed he wouldn't keep me long.

"Oh . . ." He looked back over his shoulder and smiled at me. "Congratulations. I know you're proud of BJ."

chapter eighteen

BJ was standing next to a movie poster for *High Society* when I finally pulled up in front of the Wyo Theater. Grace Kelly, hanging on Bing's and Frank's arms, reminded me of a homecoming queen in a formal dress. But BJ sure didn't look happy like Grace did.

It had gotten cold fast, so I'd put on my letter sweater. BJ was wearing my sport coat backward, with her arms through the sleeves and the opening in the back. The bottom of her pretty pink dress below the coat was flat and brownish from Nella's coffee. But it was BJ's face that worried me because she was looking terrified, pitiful—the way a kid looks before a tick shot. She didn't see me pull up, because her eyes were staring at this short pregnant lady waddling down the sidewalk. The woman reminded me of a picture in our biology book of a boa constrictor after it had swallowed a pig.

I tooted the horn. BJ didn't act like she'd heard me. Neither did the woman, who kept walking, dragging her feet along the sidewalk. I honked again. BJ kept watching the woman. I knew she had to be wondering—with our kid growing inside her—would she look that way before long. I hoped not, myself.

I left the motor running, the radio playing, and got out fast. I was halfway to the curb when she saw me. "Where have you been?" She was pissed. No wonder. "I've been standing here in the cold for forty-five minutes! Nella must have been by three times, trying to pick me up. Midge. Even Pork. Everyone in the world was worried about me but you."

"Jesus, Beej. I am so sorry. Coach got me. I couldn't get away! I did the best I could." Heard my voice get an excited tone. "Toliver may be out for Casper."

She walked right by me, opened the door to the truck, and started pulling herself in. Didn't seem glad about Toliver, either. It got pretty funny, really. Probably because her dress was wet and heavy, and with my coat's weight, she couldn't lift herself in. She'd jump up, hang on the door handle as long as she could, and try to get in, but she couldn't. Then she'd slip back down to the pavement and start again. It was hard to keep from laughing, because she wouldn't give up. She just kept trying. No upper-body strength.

I walked behind her and put my arms around her back. She went stiff. I talked into her hair. "Did you make it not getting sick? Did the coat help?" She nodded yes, but she wasn't talking. "I really am sorry, BJ."

And then a magical thing happened that turned the whole picture of us a different color. The neon movie theater lights came on over our heads. First, there was a buzz, and then flashing red and yellow. The lights warmed up the whole world where we stood underneath them. My sport coat on her shoulders wasn't brown and white; it was brown and pink. Her hair looked pink, too. The inside of the truck was all dark except for one spot on the seat, where she'd be sitting, and that spot lit up yellow, then red.

I didn't hurry to get her in the truck. Just stood behind her and leaned far enough over her back to reach her neck and kiss it. Her skin there, even though it looked red and hot in the lights, was cold on my lips. It smelled BJ-good. I swallowed a lump in my throat. She was shivering.

"I kept thinking Coach'd let me out any minute," I told her, "and then he'd remember just one more thing. All the time, I was feeling awful about you out here, waiting." Her back relaxed a little. I kissed the tickly pink hairs on the back of her neck.

"Why do things have to be so complicated for us?" She turned around to face me. Her eyes were dampish, and her mascara was smeared under one eye. Her face kept changing colors. "It should have been so simple just to pick me up on time." Red.

I lifted her up, set her on the seat. Yellow. Reached across and made sure the heater was on high, then twisted her around and kissed her on the mouth. Red. "Shit, I don't know why things go the way they do. I really tried, Beej. Does that feel some better?" I closed her door, walked around to the driver's side, and climbed into the truck.

She shivered when I got in. "Endless Sleep" came blaring out of the radio. *I saved my baby from an endless sleep.* She turned it off. "That's the original dumb song," she said. So she was talking to me again. She had my coat on normal now, opened up toward the heater. Getting warm was definitely cheering her up.

It was five twenty. I was due back at the gym at seven, so we flew out to the Bar Z. The pickup surprised me by how good it ran when I opened it up. Probably because Pork had adjusted the carburetor. When we pulled up in front of the ranch house, Buck, Mr. Bonniface's foreman, walked out the kitchen door and waved before he headed back toward the bunk house with his dog at his heels. BJ smiled and waved back. He'd worked at the Bar Z for her granddaddy before he died and now her dad. Was more family than a hand to them. Funny-looking guy, Buck. Way over six feet tall and wouldn't weigh in at over one fifty, but handsome in an old-guy way. One side of his face was a little caved in, where a bronc had landed on him, but you got used to it. Nicest, kindest man you'd ever want to meet, but he never had much to say.

BJ stayed in the truck, signaled me to do the same till he disappeared around the barn. "He wouldn't approve of you coming in with Mom and Daddy gone," she said, pushing down the door handle, "and I don't think Maria's here, either." BJ yelled, "Helloooo!" when we walked in the front door. Nobody answered, even though the lights were on and I could hear Gabriel Heatter somewhere on a radio. "C'mon." She motioned for me to follow her the other way, back to her bedroom.

So, for the first time in my life, I walked under the gun rack, past the loud-ticking grandfather clock, and down the long hall toward her bedroom. Gave me a bad case of nerves. I figured Mr. Bonniface was pissed enough already, and it wouldn't help anything if he found me back in BJ's room. But BJ was talking now and smiling, so I did what she wanted and followed her.

"It may be your only chance to invade my room in this proper household," she said, looking over her shoulder at me.

I was hoping like hell she was right that everybody else was gone.

"I've dreamed," she whispered, "about what it would be like to have you in my own bed. At least come back and talk to me while I'm getting dressed."

At the end of the hall, she stopped, rubbed herself against me, and raised up on her tiptoes to give me a kiss. It was the kind of wet, happy kiss that made my body ache for her. The kind she hadn't given me lately. "Here's my room."

"Beej, I don't think we have time." I'd noticed the clock in the hall. Five forty. We had an hour and twenty minutes to get dressed, eat, and be back at the gym. Boy, I felt stretched to my ends. "If I had fifteen more minutes," I said, following her into the dark room, "I could make your dreams come true."

I'd have known it was her room even if she didn't turn on the lights. Her lilac smell was everywhere. There were two single beds, one under each window, and the long wall to the right was full of two-handled winners' cups and ribbons she'd won in 4-H and horse shows. Only a couple weren't blue. Seemed like BJ won first place in everything she did. She was behind me then, ignoring my time worries, reaching her arms up over my shoulders, and hanging on my back, pushing her body against me. I was praying for just fifteen minutes in that room with her when it hit me.

"Beej," my voice was saying as I stripped off my letter sweater, "we've *got* fifteen extra minutes if you grab your clothes and we both dress at my place." I kicked off my shoes and unzipped my pants.

She smiled and nodded yes, her eyes sparkling. She was pulling back the spread as she stepped out of her shoes and I unzipped the back of her dress. Then she turned the lights out, pushed me backward, and was on top of me.

Her breasts in my hands, then in my mouth, seemed bigger than footballs now. For a minute, I thought about locking the door, but, Jesus, it all felt too good. The sheets were the ironed kind, cold and slippery against my back as she lowered herself down on me. For only the second time since Tomahawk Lake, we both got to feel how terrific sex can be without rubbers or anything else between you.

When she turned the light back on, the grandfather clock in the hall was just striking six. We more than had time. "You remake the bed," she said from the bathroom. "I'll throw my stuff in a suitcase."

I started worrying again as I pulled up the covers of the bed. What would happen if they caught me back here? "Hope no one sees that spot on the sheet!" I yelled to her.

She came out of the bathroom, gave me a big smile. "I may just cut it out and frame it." She was holding one of those sexy garter belts in her hand. Dropped it into her suitcase and walked back across the room to kiss me again—French-kiss me.

Mom had always said I couldn't make a decent bed if I tried, but she was wrong. This time I wanted to, and I sure did. I noticed my cigar band on the bedside table when I picked up BJ's suitcase. At least she hadn't thrown it away.

My luck had changed, I decided, when we made it back to my truck and nobody had caught us in her bedroom. We got to my place at six twenty and both got dressed, including me shaving, in under ten minutes. Mom made toasted-cheese sandwiches and vegetable soup—no milk before the game—and reminded me to take my sport coat again because I'd need it at halftime to escort Beej. BJ had on that pretty blue sweater and a straight skirt she'd pulled

143

the sweater down over because she couldn't zip it at the waist. The way her high-heel shoes made her ass stick out made me want her all over again.

I wished we had a little more time to talk to Mom. She stood at the door when we left at ten of seven, smoothing down her apron with her left hand, waving goodbye with her right. Her eyes were mushy, like melted chocolate. "If you two aren't a sight for sore eyes, I don't know who is. I'll be cheering for you at the game." She smiled. "Both of you."

"Your mom's great," BJ said as we pulled away from the curb. "So different from mine. It's like everything you do makes her happy."

We caught all three lights green on the way there and pulled in behind the school at exactly seven. I grabbed my duffel bag, told BJ I'd see her at halftime, and left her to park the truck.

"Good luck tonight!" she screamed at me out the window. "I'll be rooting for you." Just as I hit the bar to open the gym door, I remembered we hadn't talked any more about getting married. It was important to get that decided.

Pork yelled at me from his locker, "Get in here, Baby Cakes!" He smiled so big the space between his front teeth showed. "Toliver's out! Casper is history!"

chapter nineteen

H omecoming was my best game of the season. So Coach had been wrong when he said sex before a game made you weak. That extra hour I spent with him after the parade, though, he was right about that. It made all the difference because Toliver didn't play at all. Pork tore the hell out of Ralphie Smith, their second-string center, opened up holes I could drive a tractor through. Thanks to Coach, I was ready to drive.

Last play of the first half, on third and seven, I hit Ted Lackman on a flip over the middle, and he took it all the way in. First play from scrimmage in the second half, I intercepted a pass and ran it back seventy yards for another touchdown. For some reason, Coach even let me kick the extra points, which pissed the hell out of our usual kicker, that prick, Rusty Barclay. I made all four, straight through the uprights. The final score was Juniper: 28; Casper: 7. What Coach Robbins called "a decisive win."

Mr. Delaney, the scout from Wyoming, caught up with me in the locker room right after the game. He had a flat, red face with a nose the shape of those bumpy gladiola bulbs Mom makes me dig up every fall. And he was real nice. "I've heard about your circumstances, young man," he said. "Let's talk about getting engaged." He put his arm around my shoulder pads. "No need wasting your time running around, visiting other schools. We both know you belong at Wyoming." He winked at me. He had a space between his front teeth just like Pork's. "And you won't have to worry about how to pay for it, either."

Happiness shot through me. I didn't know what to do, so I just kept nodding as he said great things about me. "Yes, sir. Yes, sir." My eyes were about level with his ears. He had the biggest, reddest earlobes I'd ever seen.

Afterward, the homecoming dance in the gym was just something to get through, the usual yakking magpie girls smothering BJ, Pork hanging around to talk about the game. "God," he said. "Are we a pair or what?" I thought they all would never get lost.

Beej was feeling beat-all-to-hell tired, and me not much better. I only got racked up once on a broken play at the end of the third quarter, but it had been a long day. All we wanted to do was sit on the bottom row of the bleachers, hold hands, and talk to each other. Good luck talking with all the congratulators and The Belltones playing full blast.

"Your coat saved me from the smell today," she whispered in my ear. Her eyes looked real blue in that fuzzy sweater she was wearing. She wrinkled her nose. "But would you mind taking it off now because it's smelling a little coffee-ish every time you get close." I laughed, glad for the excuse to shuck it. Wished I had an excuse to take off the tie.

"BJ, Mr. Delaney just about guaranteed me a full football scholarship to Wyoming," I told her in a low voice.

"What?" She leaned closer. "I'm having trouble hearing you."

She was having trouble because The Belltones were now playing "Glow Worm," which had inspired Nella to organize one of those stupid bunny hop lines about a foot away from us. She was at the front of a long string of people who were jumping around and beating the hell out of the floor, even if they did have their shoes off. Nella smiled each time she passed BJ but ignored me as she hop, hop, hopped back and forth. I must have really pissed her off today. What was it I did? I couldn't remember. Oh yeah—the coffee.

BJ leaned closer to my ear. "Doesn't the gym look great? The Pep Club worked on it right up till game time." She let her head stay leaned against my shoulder.

"Yeah." I looked around. I guessed it looked as great as a gym covered in twisted crepe paper could look. There was a big spotlight on the band. Everywhere you looked, things were covered in blue and yellow. I patted her hand. "BJ, Mr. Delaney wants to give me a full scholarship to UW." I gave it a squeeze. "He says he thinks I'll be ready to start my sophomore year."

She pulled away from my shoulder, smiled up at me, but there was something sad about it. Like her mouth was too worn out from smiling all day long. "This is a chance of a lifetime for you," she said, giving me that half smile again. I couldn't blame her. Homecoming queens have to do a lot of smiling.

When Miss Cantor lowered the lights for the last dance, we stood up, and I pulled BJ up tight against me, held her the closest I ever had when we danced, but it still didn't seem tight enough. And, for the first time, I actually felt the bump in her belly between us.

She fell asleep almost the minute I got the pickup headed north to the Bar Z, her head in my lap. I had a hard time staying awake myself, even though I turned the heater off and opened the window. A yellow moon, too lopsided to bounce if it was a ball, lit up the sky. So bright you could see the whole road ahead, where it twisted up into the foothills like an unrolled ACE bandage. Which brought the game back to my mind again. I don't think I've ever felt that excited. I kept smelling the locker room, picturing myself getting taped before the game. I could remember exactly how the smack of the ball felt against my hand when I broke up that pass, how the ball hung in the air for just a second before it slid into my fingers. When I ran the whole length of the field, I never lost my wind, sucked in the cold air like I could run forever. My lucky buckeye had definitely done its work tonight. I reached in my pocket. Where was it? I'd probably left it in my jeans.

I pictured Pork blocking in front of me the fourth quarter, that hole opening up as I followed him into the end zone, still standing. Seemed now like there was a good chance we could both end up at Wyoming together on football scholarships. Mr. Delaney had noticed Pork, too. BJ made a little moaning sound in her sleep. I smoothed down her hair, and she sighed, then went quiet again.

It still surprised me that Coach had me do all the kicking. "I'm so frigging happy he let you kick," Pork said. "That son of a bitch Rusty's so stuck on himself he inspects his own asshole every time he takes a shit." I laughed out loud there in the truck, remembering. You had to admire the way Pork described things. It would really be something if we could both play together down in Laramie. I bet my ole man would show up for a game down there.

There was a taste of blood in my mouth. A little cut on my lip must have opened up again. I pulled my handkerchief out of my hip pocket. Even though her head was in my lap, BJ just kept sleeping. I pressed the handkerchief to my lip till I couldn't taste blood anymore. It didn't bother me—getting beat up and bleeding—the way it used to.

When we passed Preacher's Rock and headed into the canyon, I was still gathering back the good memories from the game. About a half mile from BJ's gate, I passed their bull pasture. A bull was following a fat Hereford cow, his nose to her tail. Talk about hung. Bulls have got the market cornered on being hung. I knew from watching him before that he'd follow her all night till he wore her out. I admired that about bulls.

BJ was sleeping so hard that I had to shake her when we stopped in front of the ranch house. She pretty much sleep-walked toward the front door, me guiding her the whole way. I kissed her good night, had opened the door for her to go in when I remembered. I pushed her away from me so she'd have to look at my face, put one hand on each of her shoulders inside her open coat. Her bones under the blue sweater were so little they felt like bird bones. "I want you to wake up and pay attention to me," I said. "This is important."

She yawned, raised her eyebrows up under her bangs, but her eyes didn't quite open. Her eyelashes were so long that they never seemed quite real.

"BJ! Listen! I mean it. I don't want you to do anything stupid till we talk again. Okay?"

She shivered, so I pulled my hands out and buttoned her coat. Finally, she nodded. "Mom says I have to stay home and rest all day tomorrow, anyway." She smiled up at me. "So there's nothing for you to worry about. You know I'm safe here. Call me, though, will you?"

"Sure thing."

The light by the door made little angel halos over the top of her head when I bent down to kiss her again, but her yawn got in my way.

"I'm hopeless," she said. "Too tired to even kiss you right. It's been such a good day, Rob. Let's do something after church on Sunday, maybe just walk down by the river or saddle up Belle and Biscuit and go for a ride in the mountains."

"Deal," I said, as she turned to walk in the door. "And, BJ?"

She stopped right under the light and looked up at me, her short brown hair looking so shiny and beautiful. "What, Rob?"

"BJ, I love you better than anything."

Her smile back was the good kind. "I love you better."

chapter twenty

P ork's call on Saturday woke me at noon. "C'mon," he said. "There's a new movie on at the Wyo that's going to help me explore my career options. I saved your ass last night. You owe me."

I met him thirty minutes later in front of the theater. The frizzy-haired lady in the ticket booth frowned at his Pervert hat but sold us tickets anyway. We saw *The Fiend Who Walked the West* two times. Movies are great. They take over your mind, uncomplicate things. Even the music helps. You don't get caught off guard, can relax till drums start or the music turns scary. Then you sit up straight and look out. Better than real life for knowing when trouble's coming, that's for sure.

It was great to kick back. We ate till our money ran out: four boxes of buttered popcorn, a couple of Butterfingers, a box of Jordan Almonds, and a gallon of Coke. I didn't get home till five thirty, and then I dialed BJ's number.

Her mother answered. "She's been stir-crazy all day, Rob, but I've kept her in bed, and she looks better already. Say, congratulations on a great game. BJ told me about your scholarship offer. You had quite a day yesterday!" Her voice was excited for me. Sometimes Mrs. Bonniface could be so nice. Maybe BJ was right: it all depended on the booze. I was betting Mrs. Bonniface wouldn't be that friendly if she knew about the kid.

"Well, could I talk to her for just a minute, Mrs. Bonniface? I won't take long. It's great she's feeling better."

She sighed into the phone. "She's not here. She wore me down, said if I'd give her just thirty minutes to walk down by the river, she'd come back and stay in bed the rest of the day." I heard her take in another breath. "Oh, Rob, I almost forgot. BJ said if you called while she was gone, I was to tell you not to come out after church tomorrow. She and her father are cooking up something, and she wasn't sure when they'd be through. She'll call you."

"Okay," I said, noticing that flapping-bird feeling had come back in my chest. My voice didn't sound quite right. "Okay, Mrs. Bonniface. But today, would you make sure she calls me just the minute she comes back from the river?"

"We'll see." Her voice wasn't as friendly. "BJ may need a day off, Rob. She really needs to rest."

Oh brother. In my house, that meant no. My throat went tight around my Adam's apple. What in the hell should I do? I seriously needed to talk to Beej.

"By the way," she said, "have you by any chance remembered what happened to that glass deer eye?"

Great. We were off on another subject. "Yes, I think so, Mrs. Bonniface. I'm pretty sure BJ put it in the pocket of that yellow coat just as I was leaving."

"Hmm. Well, she didn't remember that. It's not in her coat pocket. The yellow one is mine. Maria and I've looked everywhere. The eyes are antiques, a pair Don's father bought in England, so I can't replace just the one."

Shit, I had to talk to BJ. "Sure wish I could help you more, Mrs. Bonniface. Check the yellow coat. Listen, it's real, real important for me to talk to your daughter. Please have her call me back."

But BJ didn't call, even though I stayed home Saturday night and lied to Pork about why. A whole night in the house with your mother, Lawrence Welk, and his bubble machine doesn't exactly lead to a peaceful state of mind. By eight o'clock, I was fucking nuts.

Just before nine, I broke down and called the Bar Z again. Mrs. Bonniface answered, and this time she sounded mad, her words running together. "Rob, BJ's in bed asleep, and I have no intention of waking her. There are times a mother has to put her foot down." I heard the sound of ice in a glass, like she was taking a drink. Then a big sigh. "Even if she's not appreciated for doing it."

"Yes, Mrs. Bonniface. Well, I'm real sorry to bother you."

"She'll call you as soon as it's convenient." Click. Did Mrs. Bonniface know now?

I went back into the living room with Mom, thudded down beside her on the couch.

"Great news," Mom said. "There's a Lawrence Welk special tonight, two straight hours!" More sappy music, dancing couples, church-faced women with matching hairdos. Everybody—even the guys with their slicked-back hair—smiled out of the TV at me like I should be happy because they were.

"Robbie," Mom said, "stop squirming. If you don't like Lawrence Welk, go upstairs and listen to your own music."

So I did. Went up there, shut the door, took off my shoes and socks, and turned my radio up loud on KOMA. It was the only station we got that played current hits—and then, only at night—clear from Oklahoma. At least it drowned out the sound of Lawrence Welk in my head.

How could I get to BJ? I stretched out on my bed and stared at my feet. Noticed that little black hairs were growing on top of both my big toes, which is the last thing I remember.

+ + +

I was still dressed when I woke up the next morning. Mom had thrown the big quilt over me again. Guess I was tireder than I'd thought. I begged out of church by showing her some new bruises on my arm and the scab on my mouth. She didn't make me do stuff if she thought I was hurt. "You deserve a good rest after the week you've had." *Boy*, I thought as she pulled the veil down on her hat, *if she only knew.* "Help yourself to lunch. I left you some stew. I'll be back soon as I can get the flowers off the altar."

I sat by the phone all morning, afraid I'd really piss off Mrs. Bonniface if I called BJ again. I even tried staring at the phone for a while. Maybe looking at it long enough would make it ring. But it just stared back at me with its dial like an empty eye. Finally, I took my notebook to the kitchen table near the phone and tried working on my now-very-late Shakespeare paper. Didn't make any difference whether I sat there or not. Nobody called.

Time went dragging on. *If I was in a movie*, I thought, *the get-worried music would be playing.* Mom picked up on it when she came home from church, carrying an armful of bright-orange flowers that made me sneeze. "You haven't eaten two bites of your lunch, Robbie. You didn't get hurt worse than you told me, did you?"

I shook my head no, fighting back the urge to spill my guts to her, and sneezed.

She set the flowers on the table, frowned, and twirled a curled-up tip of her hair around one finger. "Is something bothering you?"

"No, Mom. It's okay. Just this cut on my mouth. It's hard to talk. I gotta go back to my room. I'm allergic to those flowers."

By four thirty, I couldn't take it any longer. Figured the hell with Mrs. Bonniface and called BJ again. No answer. Not Maria, Mrs. Bonniface, Buck, Mr. Bonniface, nobody. Then my movie music went from nervous to sit-up-straight-and-be-awful-scared. I had to get to BJ. It felt like there was a bomb ticking inside me.

Mom was sitting on the couch again when I walked through the living room. I tried to act like it was no big deal. "Think I'll mosey out to the Bar Z and track down Beej, Mom. We were supposed to get together today, and maybe I missed something."

She put down her knitting and stared at me, then ran her hand through her bangs like she does when she's worried. "You sure there's not something we need to talk about?"

I shook my head no, grabbed my coat, and sprinted out the door. When her eyes go all soft, it gets to me. Tears were stinging my own eyes. I reached for my buckeye in my jeans pocket. No buckeye there, either. Shit. Where was it?

I felt better to be in the truck, heading BJ's way. It was trying to snow out west but wasn't cold enough yet. So the mist rose up over the mountains in little puffs like smoke

155

from a hundred cabins you couldn't see. Not many cars on the road.

I passed Lloyd's Esso station in Big Horn, turned right toward the mountains. I'd be fine if I could just see her.

It was a dark, gloomy day. I felt as little as an ant driving through Tongue River Canyon, its walls towering up above me. A solid-yellow no-passing line ran clear through the canyon because the road was so narrow. I didn't see another car till I came out at the other end. A beat-up red Caddie veered away, then straightened out and fishtailed into the canyon back the way I'd come. The fastest I'd ever seen a car go on that road. Doc Justice was the only person I knew with a Caddie that color.

I automatically looked right at the old Franklin place for the little herd of antelope by the windmill there. Sure enough, there they were, but their heads were all looking back up the road behind me after the Caddie. Guess they weren't used to seeing a car flying low, either.

The wind had picked up, making whistling noises around the cab of the pickup. It was starting to snow, too, the hard pellet kind that bounces off the windshield. I drove on, thinking how lonely wind could sound. Wondered where Doc was going in such a hurry. That damn song BJ hated came back in my head: *I took your baby from you away.* God, I needed to touch her. Everything would be all right then. I was going to get this marriage thing straightened out once and for all. It had been put off too long.

I couldn't help laughing when I saw the bull in the pasture before the Bonnifaces' gate. He was humping that fat red cow. Looked like it took him all weekend, but he had her now, and the snow wasn't bothering him one bit.

I hit the cattle guard so hard it knocked my foot off the gas. Was going faster than I'd realized. I got my balance back, gave it more gas, and noticed fresh tire tracks on the muddy snow in the road there. Somebody had just come or gone from the ranch. I couldn't see the top of the little cemetery hill; it was whited-out by the storm blowing in.

When I rounded the corner by the barn, I saw Mrs. Bonniface's gray Lincoln parked in front of the house, and the gate in the fence was wide open. Someone was standing in the yard, staring down the drive in my direction. God, I prayed it was BJ. When I got close, though, I saw it was Mrs. Bonniface, there alone in the blowing snow. She wouldn't like me showing up uninvited and not calling first. I'd never done that before.

I pulled to a stop in front and waited to see what she'd do. She didn't do anything. Mrs. Bonniface had the look of a frozen statue of herself: no blinking, no smiling, just her staring back up the drive past the barn and barely holding her own in the wind. All the color was drained out of her. She didn't have on even a coat or a sweater—just a short-sleeve white shirt with a red-and-white-checkered kitchen towel stuck in the front of her jeans like an apron.

I turned off the engine and decided to get out. All of a sudden, I felt more worried about her than about her being pissed at me. I slammed the pickup door, ran through the gate to her without closing it. "Mrs. Bonniface! Are you okay?"

She jumped. "Oh, Rob," she said. "I'm glad you're here. Something awful has happened to BJ. Doc Justice and Don just left with her." Mrs. Bonniface's eyes were as big as silver dollars.

"What? What happened to her?" Mrs. Bonniface didn't answer, but her face said it was real bad. Something inside me cracked into pieces like a window I once hit dead center when my line drive went fly. I had to get to BJ! I had to! "I'll find them, Mrs. Bonniface. I think I passed them back at the mouth of the canyon. Doesn't Doc have a red Caddie?"

She nodded, but grabbed my hand, her fingers cold as sled runners. "Wait. Don't go. There's nothing you can do." Her face was a funny blue color.

"I have to, Mrs. Bonniface. I gotta get to BJ." I dropped her hand and sprinted back to my pickup. Had already opened the door and climbed in behind the wheel when I saw her teeter, then fall to her knees. Somehow I made it back in time to catch her before she hit the ground. Her teeth were chattering. "I think she's gone, Rob. Doc said she was dead."

"Dead? Who? BJ?"

She nodded yes.

BJ, dead? For a minute, I lost all my understanding, couldn't get the meaning to sink in my head, couldn't catch my breath in the swirling snow. I had to get to BJ. But Mrs. Bonniface said she was dead? My knees felt like they were about to buckle, too.

I practically gasped it out. "Mrs. Bonniface, how could BJ be dead?"

She pointed to the house. "Let's get out of this wind, talk in there."

I walked her inside and sat down by her on the leather couch across from the one-eyed deer head. Midnight, BJ's black cat, jumped in her lap and began rubbing his head into her shirtfront. I was still trying to figure out how to breathe. Mrs. Bonniface didn't look like she cared if she did. She didn't seem to notice Midnight, just kept staring at the deer head, tears pouring down her face.

There was a little fire left in the fireplace. I got up and threw a couple of logs on it, tried to stir it, but it didn't much want to burn. I couldn't get my bearings on what to do. "Mrs. Bonniface," I said, "please tell me where they took her, what happened. I want to be with her."

Her voice answered me strong for as bad as she looked. "Rob, there's really nothing either one of us can do now. I need you here. Please stay till Don gets back. They'll call when they know something, and I wouldn't even know where to tell you to look for them." She shook her head from side to side like she couldn't believe it, either, and then began crying so hard her shoulders heaved up and down.

Jesus, I didn't know how to help her, how to help myself. I patted her back, racking my brain to think what Mom would do if she was here.

"Okay," I finally said, my voice sounding strangled when it came out of my mouth. "Okay, Mrs. Bonniface. What if I make us some hot chocolate? I always feel better when my mom makes hot chocolate. And cold as you are, you need some. First, though, could you try and tell me what's happened?"

She caught her breath. "It was a wasp sting, hornet . . . something down in the barn." Mrs. Bonniface's red eyes wouldn't look into mine, so I didn't quite believe her. "She must have had an allergic reaction," she was saying. "You know, like her daddy. Don almost died from a beesting once. He gave her two shots of his adrenaline, but it was too late." Tears poured down her cheeks. I dug in my pocket for my handkerchief and gave it to her. She took it but still wouldn't look at me.

She *had* to know about my kid now. What she was saying made no sense at all. My head was pounding as I tried to sort out what I should say to her and what I shouldn't. "A wasp?" I finally said. "A wasp in October? BJ got stung out at Tomahawk Lake last summer, and nothing like that happened."

Mrs. Bonniface pushed the cat out of her lap, stood up, and walked around the couch to the big windows, staring out at Mount Quandary. But she didn't answer me. Finally, she turned around, pulled the checked towel out from her jeans, and wiped her face off with it. "Well," she said, her voice real hard, "it did this time."

A big gust of wind rattled the windows. A huge gray cloud moved over the top of Mount Quandary, and the whole living room went dark. Snow was beginning to stick to the tops of fence posts out beyond the yard. The fire was dying out. I didn't know what else to say. I was sure now that she knew about the baby, but she wasn't talking to me about it.

Mrs. Bonniface folded up the checked towel, set it on an end table, and turned back to the windows. She wrapped both her arms around her sides, hugging herself the exact same way BJ did when she felt afraid.

Something inside me wanted to sob out so bad.

Then her whole body began to shake. The cat was worried. He began winding around her legs, rubbing against her, and meowing. Mrs. Bonniface was crying so hard now she had to steady herself on the window frame.

I went over and put my arm around her shoulders. The feel of her bones led my memory straight back to BJ. I swallowed, swallowed again, and steered her back over to the couch. "Here, Mrs. Bonniface." I patted the seat. "You lie down now, and I'll cover you up. You're plumb frozen." I picked up the big bison robe off the back of the couch and laid it over her. "I'll make you some hot chocolate." Her eyes looked relieved. She nodded. "You just stay put," I told her.

"Call Maria," she whispered. "She'll help you. Oh, that's right—it's Sunday." She tried to stand up.

"It's all right, Mrs. Bonniface. I can do it."

I found sugar and the cocoa in the pantry, pulled a saucepan out of the shelf by the range, guesstimated six tablespoons of cocoa the way Rose had taught me. My hands shook when I dumped it into the pan, then went to the fridge to get the milk.

I opened the door. What the hell? There in the fridge door was Mr. Bonniface's bee sting medicine. I picked up the little bottle that was labeled adrenaline. It was completely full. The seal wasn't even broken.

chapter twenty-one

LARAMIE, WYOMING

April 6, 1961

"U h, Nella?"

I knew Rob's voice on the phone, but I wasn't going to act like it. "Yes?"

"Hi, it's Rob. I'm calling for a funny reason."

"Oh, hi back, Rob." I motioned my sorority sisters away from the phone booth in our entry hall. "Haven't seen you since the mixer. So I guess any reason's a funny one. What can I do for you?"

"Well, actually"—I still loved his gruff, boyish voice—"it's what *I* can do for you. Your dad called and left a message for me at the SAE house."

"My dad?"

"Yeah, I just got back from football practice and saw it. See, I'm working out with the varsity this spring. A storm's headed south, lots of heavy wet snow. It's already breaking fences and trees up in Montana, blocking roads. He wants me to drive you and Midge home for spring break in your car. Tomorrow morning. Midge's supposed to blow off Good Friday mass."

"Nice of him to talk to me about this."

"Ah, Nella, don't be a prick. I'm just doing what he asked me to."

"That's what I like about you, Rob—always doing your duty."

Silence.

"Well, sure." I gave in first. "If you're willing to drive, come on by the Kappa house about seven. You can leave your truck here." The thought of being locked in a car with him for six full hours made me nervous.

"Seven's, uh, too early," he said. "I've got . . . uh . . . something going on tonight. And the transmission's shot in my pickup. Pork's working on it right now. So why don't you and Midge leave the Kappa house about ten, swing by, and pick me up?"

"Ten seems a little late, if we're trying to beat a storm to Juniper. Oh, and, Rob, Midge isn't riding with me now. Change of plans. She's going to Denver with Mike to see his sister." I didn't believe that part of her story for a minute.

Silence.

"Okay, well, sure, Nella. We can still go." He didn't sound happy. "But no way I can leave before ten. Pick me up at ten."

I bet if he'd known Midge wasn't coming, he wouldn't have even called unless he needed the ride.

After BJ's death a year and a half ago, everything had— as Midge described it—"gone to shit." Poof! Like a popped balloon, my mighty senior confidence dissipated. Things felt flat and surreal, everything different, but no one talking about it.

Rob, of course, had continued to avoid me. Rusty took his ring back without comment and was going steady with Lorna Casey before the month was over. When I told Mom the story about BJ and the bee sting at Tomahawk Lake, she'd looked alarmed, put down her dish towel, and come to sit beside me at the kitchen table. "You've got to promise me, Nella, not to mention this to anyone else. There's clearly more to this story than the Bonnifaces want people to know. Please keep this secret for BJ's sake." Turns out, Midge's mother told her the exact same thing. So Midge and I, who were both quite sure that a beesting had not killed BJ, could only talk about it to each other.

Miss Cantor had even called us back to her office at the start of the spring semester to reinforce how important it was to keep setting that good example. Everyone's senior year didn't need to be ruined. "I don't want you to allow yourself to be morose about BJ, girls. We will face our loss quietly and show our character by not imposing our feelings on our classmates." Those last months of high school, Midge and I sleepwalked through a nightmare from which we could not awake.

So I'd really been ready to leave Juniper and start fresh in Laramie last fall. And it had gone even better than I'd hoped. I'd made good new friends, loved my classes and—best of all—left my sad-secret-keeping BJ world behind. I was nervous about tomorrow, though. Rob had blown me off every time I'd tried to talk to him about what had happened to BJ, but I was pretty sure he knew. And now, thanks to my dad, I was about to be locked in the car alone with him all day. At least, at last, maybe I would finally learn the truth

+++

He was ten minutes late coming out of the SAE house the next morning, and I sure wasn't comfortable going in to get him. I waited in the passenger seat of my convertible with the top up and heater running, getting madder and more nervous by the minute. *Is he just not going to show?*

When he finally did come out, the sun was still shining, but ominous gray storm clouds were gathering in the northern sky. He was wearing a shiny new brown-and-yellow UW letter jacket, had a sloppily rolled sleeping bag slung over one shoulder, and was carrying a duffel. As little attention as I paid to football, even I knew he'd been the star quarterback on the freshman team last fall. He looked taller and bigger all over than the last time I'd seen him almost three months ago.

He was chewing something when he walked up to my window. I rolled it down. "Hi," he said, "take this." He handed me a greasy paper napkin covering something purple. "I brought six extra pieces of toast in case we get hungry. Three buttered, and three have grape jelly. Help yourself." He stepped back and eyeballed my baby-blue convertible.

"It was my high school graduation present."

"Guess you don't miss the ole Jeep now. Not a bad deal, your ole man bein' in the car business." He stooped to look in the back seat. "You got chains in the trunk?" I nodded. "We'll put 'em on later. They slow you down on the blacktop."

He walked to the driver's side, opened the back door, and threw in his duffel, the sleeping bag, and his letter jacket. Then he opened the driver's door, slid in behind the steering wheel, and adjusted the seat as far back as it would go. His presence—his sheer bigness—pretty much filled up my car. I didn't know what to do with the greasy napkin full of toast. Anyplace I put it would leave a stain.

"Automatic transmission." He frowned, then backed out of the parking space twice as fast as I would have. "Me, I like a manual in the snow."

He had on aftershave. Bay Rum, maybe? I liked it. He was unshaven and looked hungover, like he'd just climbed out of bed. Something that looked like egg was stuck to the whiskers on his top lip. There was sleep sand in his eyes, and his wavy, uncombed dark hair stuck out at crazy angles. His blue button-down collar shirt was wrinkled, his shirttail out and one collar button undone. *So*, I wondered, *why did he put on the aftershave?*

"You've got egg on your mouth." I'd want somebody to tell me.

He scowled. "Anything else wrong? Go ahead and make you a list so we can get it all over at once." He pulled the car to a stop at the last traffic light in Laramie.

"Well, now that you mention it . . ." I pushed a strand of hair out of my eye and tucked it behind my ear. I'd been to a stylist in Denver, who'd cut my hair in a long bob that actually made me look pretty. "There's lots to talk about, Rob—don't you think?"

"Just let me wake up, will you?" He turned onto the straight, open highway that headed north. "I'm not up for anything heavy this morning." He cut on the radio. One of the new twist songs was playing. Then he pulled a pair of sunglasses out of his shirt pocket, shoved them onto his nose, slumped down in his seat, and looked as unfriendly as a guy could look. I got the message. As messy and grumpy as he looked, though, I still felt an undercurrent of attraction for him. That same old sexual attraction, if I was honest with myself.

He didn't say ten words the next two hours, just kept flipping the radio dial, whistling to himself, and chewing toast. I sang along with the radio when I knew the songs: "Mack the Knife," "Till There Was You," "Itsy Bitsy Teenie Weenie Yellow Polka Dot Bikini." I wished I knew all the words like I had back in high school.

The wind picked up between Laramie and Medicine Bow, where the grass was depressingly brown and the landscape stark and barren. Occasionally, a tumbleweed came hurling by or a cold blast of wind shook the car. I buttoned up my cardigan, wished my parka wasn't back in the trunk, and turned up the heater. I should have worn jeans instead of my new wool kilt to try to impress him.

Why, after all these years, do I still care what Rob thinks?

He rolled his shirtsleeves up above his elbows, unbuttoned two buttons on his shirt, and cracked the window. I couldn't help noticing how huge his arms had gotten. Rocky Marciano arms.

A few minutes later, without a word to me, he reached over and turned off my heater.

Geez, I was freezing. "You care if I borrow your sleeping bag, Rob? I'm getting a little chilly."

"Help yourself," he said. "That bag is *my* graduation present. From Rose and Carl, my sister and her ole man. It's pretty warm. Army surplus, oversize."

I'd ended up putting his toast on the cardboard back of a steno notebook and setting it on the dashboard. Twice, he'd asked for another piece—once with, once without jelly. His fingers were warm on my icy ones when I touched him. The too-sweet smell of grapes made me nauseous. I wished I didn't have such a sensitive stomach. I turned down the radio to make conversation. "Who'll be at your house over break?"

"Mom."

"Do you ever see your dad?" Everyone in Juniper knew the story about Mr. Hitchcock.

Rob shifted in his seat. "I think I saw him two times, in the bleachers at games. Rose is pretty sure he was at homecoming our senior year. Remember that good game I had against Casper?"

What I remember is that was the last day I saw BJ alive. I wonder if it was the last day he did, too.

"But my ole man never shows up afterward." Rob's mouth twitched in an ironic half grin. "Put it this way: I'm not looking to get a convertible from him anytime soon."

"I'm sorry, Rob. That must be so tough."

He nodded quietly.

I couldn't think of what to say to him next. *It never used to be that way with us.* "Rumor has it, Mike's giving Midge an engagement ring in June." Mike and Rob were both SAEs.

"Girls know more about that shit than me. I don't see much of Mike these days." He turned the radio back up.

It had started spitting snow. We were heading into the long stretch between Douglas and Wheatland, the most desolate part of the drive. Not another car in sight. I wondered if it wasn't time to put the chains on, but he'd be irritated if I suggested it. I waited till an instrumental, "Theme of

Exodus," came on to try to talk to him again. "Have you decided on a major yet?" *Geez, Nella. Could you ask a more inane question?*

"I have." He answered like he was surprised at himself, the look on his face not so sour. "I think I'm gonna coach. You know, with the situation with my ole man, Coach Robbins made all the difference in my chances. Besides, I like kids, and I think I'd be okay at teaching them how to play ball." He nodded toward the pile of toast, and I dodged the grape smell by handing him a buttered piece.

"That's so cool! You would really be a great coach." A turkey buzzard flew across the road up ahead. It landed on an antelope carcass beside the road, furiously flapping its huge wings to stay upright in the strong, gusty wind. "I wish I'd decided on a major. If I make it through organic chemistry, I'm considering premed. Can you imagine me, a woman doctor? I met one at the infirmary last fall when I had mono. Evidently, med schools are admitting more girls now."

He didn't answer, was watching the buzzard, whose head was completely inside the carcass as we drove past. The carcass was covered with snow now, and so was the highway. It was a miracle to me that Rob could tell where the road was.

So far, I'd had plenty of quiet thinking time on this trip. With the mood he was in, it was definitely not the time to bring up BJ. Something else that had worried me for over four years was niggling at me again. After about three hours, I decided I didn't have much to lose, so I brought it up. "You want to know something, Rob? I've never forgotten that night our freshman year with you in Calvin's car out by the girls' school."

"You haven't?" He looked confused. "How come?"

"Because I'd never gone that far with a guy before, let alone a guy I wasn't even dating. I've felt guilty ever since. BJ treated me really weird homecoming week, and it made me wonder if maybe you hadn't finally told her about it."

"We went that far, you and me? Shit, that's big news. But you got no worries there. We had a Bohingi Boy meeting that night, and I was so sloshed I can't remember much of anything." He smiled, his first real smile of the trip, and chewed the egg off his top lip with his lower teeth. "Wish I did, though. Sounds worth remembering." He smoothed his hair down with his free hand and gave me a suggestive look. "Exactly just how far did we go?" One lock of his hair was still sticking up, like Dennis the Menace.

I felt a blush creep up my neck. "Farther than we should have. Farther than I've gone with any guy before or since." *So if he didn't tell BJ, why was she so mad at me?*

"You're kidding! Farther than you and Rusty?" He turned and looked me up and down. "I'm impressed. You're right about Beej. She'd have been royally pissed. Maybe it's a good thing I don't remember, or I'd feel even shittier than I already do." He smiled sadly.

I felt disgusted with myself all over again and sighed. A really big blast of wind hit the car so hard it pushed us off on the shoulder. Some red long johns whipped off a clothesline by a shacky house there and blew under our right front tire. I jerked back in my seat, but Rob just steered us back to the middle of the road with one hand.

He's a good driver. I'm really glad I'm not driving in this weather.

"Here comes your storm, Nella. We're picking up a real headwind." He pointed toward the roiling, darkening sky ahead. "Maybe you were right—we shoulda left a little earlier. There's an Esso station on this side of Casper with cheap gas. Let's stop there. I want a full tank heading into this stuff. You got gas money? Your ole man said to ask you."

I nodded yes.

"Good. I'll throw the chains on there."

Hard to believe he actually admitted he was wrong for a change. The sky ahead did look seriously threatening. I shivered. At least I could get my parka out of the trunk and buy a cup of hot chocolate in Casper.

After he'd gassed up, put the chains on, and we were back on the road, Rob finally rolled up his window. It looked like he'd washed his face and combed his hair in the men's room. I'd actually put on a little pink lipstick myself, and bought some Hershey's bars with what was left of my gas money. Heavier snow was pelting our windshield now and collecting on the blacktop. The wipers were so crusted with ice that they scraped as they moved back and forth. Rob had to lean close to the windshield to see, but he still seemed completely confident. And competent. *My dad knew what he was doing when he asked him to do this.*

Rob straightened us out of yet another skid and cleared his throat. "Now, listen to this, Nella. Here's a story about a real storm." There had been a five-day snowstorm in the forties, Rob said. It had hit while his dad was hunting in the Bighorn Mountains. The snow had gotten so deep that people had to string rope between their houses and barns to find their way and gather eggs as soon as they were laid or they'd freeze solid. Rob's dad's neighbor had seen his mongrel dog blown clean out of his doghouse.

"These are not reassuring stories." I clamped my hand over his mouth to stop him from talking, felt an unexpected rush when my fingers touched his lips, and quickly returned my hand to my paper hot chocolate cup. "I do *not* want to hear any more about how bad it can get."

He laughed his wonderful, spontaneous laugh, and I relaxed a little. It might be freezing outside, but things were finally warming up with us here in the car.

"We'll be okay, Nella. I brought the Womb."

"The Womb?"

He pointed at the sleeping bag draped over my lap. "I remembered my ole man's story, so I came prepared."

chapter twenty-two

The blizzard had really slowed us down. We were still thirty miles from Juniper at five o'clock when Rob began pumping the brakes and stopped the car. "There's something up ahead. I better have a look." He'd spotted it through a windshield so snow-crusted I hadn't seen a thing. He threw on his letter jacket and stepped out of the car, his dark hair and lashes immediately frosting with snow as he disappeared into a wall of white.

When he reopened the car door, stomping his boots before sliding back in, he was frowning. "Well, we're stuck." He rubbed his head with a bare hand and dumped about a quart of wet snow all over my new car's front seat. "I coulda got us home easy, but there's a damn snowplow broken down up there, with a three-foot drift blocking the whole frigging highway." He turned off the ignition. "We can't keep the car running. We'll need gas to warm up every now and then, and to get us to Juniper. Remind me to keep an eye on your car roof. Too much heavy snow piled up there could tear your canvas top." He smiled and pointed at the last piece of grape toast on the dashboard. "At least we got food."

"You are more than welcome to that entire piece your-self," I said. "And I will share these!" With a flourish, I produced the four Hershey's bars I'd bought in Casper. His face lit up when I handed him one. "So, Rob, since we're not going to starve to death, what's going to keep us from freezing?"

"No worries there." He exuded a confidence I sure didn't feel as he finished the candy bar in two bites. "We still have three-quarters of a tank. That's enough to turn the heater off and on every now and then. Mostly, though, we're gonna have to depend on body heat." He threw me a crooked smile. "We'll put the Womb on the back seat and get in together."

I gulped, not at all sure how I'd handle being pressed up against him in a sleeping bag. Just in case he suspected how nervous I was, I quickly changed the subject. "What about that toast? Shouldn't you eat it now like the chicken eggs?"

He knew I was teasing, laughed, and grabbed the sleeping bag off my lap, unzipping one side before he lobbed it onto the back seat. "You may be glad for your half of that toast come morning, little girl. And I'm damn sure I'll be glad for your Hershey's bars." He swept his hand toward the back seat, like it was my turn to go first down a plush red carpet. "Ladies first—and don't worry. I'll be the perfect gentleman."

So he knew what I was thinking.

It took about five minutes for the two of us to awkwardly maneuver ourselves into the sleeping bag. By then, I was shivering uncontrollably, so he put his arms around me, which warmed me up in more ways than one. His body put out heat like a radiator. When he pulled the zipper clear up, we were smashed together, my back to his front. His closeness and the warmth of the sleeping bag heightened his intoxicating smells. So there I was, cosmically attracted to

Rob Hitchcock and no way to escape. *Think about something else, Nella. Anything else.*

When my teeth stopped chattering, we made awkward small talk for a while, but I finally decided that this would be the best chance I'd ever have to find out what had happened to BJ. So I raised the subject. "Why will you never talk to me about BJ, Rob?" At least this time, he couldn't just turn around and leave, like he did when I'd asked him in a quiet corner at the Kappa–SAE mixer.

But he could stonewall me. "I can't talk about it, Nella."

This time I was *not* going to let it drop. "I really need to know what happened, Rob. She was my best friend. It nags at me all the time."

He changed the subject. "I'm kicking myself for forgetting that Bohingi Boy night! But I'm not the same guy now that I was then. Losing BJ changed me—or I'd already be trying to figure out how to bang you here in this sleeping bag."

We both laughed. I took a deep breath to fight off a tidal wave of feelings. Warm tears flooded my eyes. "You'll always be hers to me, Rob. I'm actually glad it didn't go any further between us. Can't we at least talk about what happened to her? We both know it wasn't a wasp sting." I twisted around to face him, my kilt riding above my knees. At least it put a little more space between our hips. I put my hands on each side of his icicle-cold cheeks and held his face so he couldn't look away. His hair was dripping melted snow. "Rob, it eats on me all the time, not knowing the truth." A major, scary gust of wind—the biggest so far—shook the car. Dark was falling fast.

"I don't know *all* of what happened." He lowered his head out of my hands. "But I've got a pretty good idea about it. Jesus, I *need* to know, too, Nella. It messes with my head. I tried to do right and marry her."

"Marry BJ? What do you mean? Why would you marry her?" My breasts were so smashed into his chest that I could feel the boom, boom, booming of his heart.

"Shit, I knew if I talked long enough, I'd let the cat out of the bag. Me and my damn big mouth."

Finally, I was learning something that made sense. "I won't tell anyone. I promise."

Outside the car, a bitter blast of snow extinguished the last of the light, and the blizzard completely enveloped us. It was now impossible to see his face, so I waited in the long silence that followed, thinking he was probably finished talking about her. But then he took a deep breath and let it out.

"Maybe it's the right thing to tell you since you were BJ's best friend. Shit, I don't know what to do. I hope this makes sense." His heart was beating faster now. "You can't ever tell anyone this. *Ever!* She was going to have a kid, Nella—my kid. She wasn't pissed at you. She was just sick as a dog and scared shitless." A sob caught in his throat. "I thought we had it all settled, getting married. We'd have been all right. Her mom didn't know anything, but her ole man went bonkers. Said BJ was underage and he'd never sign for her to marry me. He was looking all over for someone to give her an abortion."

My heart began to hammer then. I found myself crazily wondering if they'd tried Midge's pop-bottle idea.

"He got BJ talked into one, is my best guess. She wasn't excited about having a kid, either." I could tell Rob was crying. I wrapped my arms around him. "She didn't call, and she didn't call all day." His voice cracked. "So I finally just drove out to the ranch, but shit, just like with everything but football, my timing was off. By the time I got there, she was gone—already dead, I think—in Doc's car with her dad. Honest to God, Nella, he never told me what happened. I know one thing: his bee sting medicine—you know, that shot stuff her ole man keeps in the icebox?—it was still there. Whatever killed her, you're right—it wasn't a wasp. And think about this: the Bonnifaces do all their burying in that cemetery up on the hill, even their dogs. So why would they pay people in Billings to burn BJ up and not just bury her there?"

I was shaking uncontrollably now. And I was desperate to find words, any words, that might comfort him. Too many all came tumbling out at once. "It sounds like you did everything you could, Rob. You were giving up a lot to get married that young. Nobody in the world would have been able to change their minds if BJ and her dad both decided to do something." I flashed back to the Thomas Dewey Parade, that giant man with his determined, tiny daughter who didn't want to march in the parade, so she wasn't made to do it. "They were a pair. If BJ and Mr. Bonniface both didn't want her having a baby, they probably did something to be sure she didn't."

"I should have stood up to him stronger, Nella. Asked BJ more questions about what they were thinking." Rob's chest was heaving. "Anyway, it doesn't really matter, because the whole goddamned thing was my fault. I as much as killed her. First, I didn't wear a rubber and knocked her up. And then I got busy as a cat covering crap, thinking about my big football game and Bohingi Boy initiation and a lot of other shit when I should have focused my mind on Beej." Rob sighed. "It was all my fault, my goddamned stupid fault!" His cries became anguished, agonizing sobs.

"You're wrong. *Really wrong.*" I couldn't let him carry this whole burden. I burrowed my face into the hard muscles of his shoulder and tried to clear my head. "You're kind. You're hardworking. You're well meaning. You're honest. You just got caught in a terrible buzz saw. BJ and her dad made whatever decision was made, not you. Don't be so hard on yourself. BJ wouldn't want that."

I felt for his face in the dark, mopped his tears with my mittened hand, and kissed his cheek as my own heart splintered into a thousand pieces of its own regret. *Why didn't I see that something was so wrong? Why was I so hateful to her when she needed me the most?* And then I was crying, too. For Rob, for myself—but most of all, for my dearest and best dead friend. Once begun, Rob and I had a lot of mourning to do. We really couldn't offer each other much in the way of assuaging guilt, but his physical presence, his patiently holding me and his understanding how I felt, helped me finally begin the long process of letting BJ go. Eventually, I was so exhausted from crying that I forgot the storm, the howling gusts rocking the car, and relaxed into the strength and heat of him. We fell asleep holding each other while outside of my little car, the fierce Wyoming blizzard raged on.

The next morning, I awoke first to anemic yellow rays of sun streaking the eastern sky. The storm had finally blown itself out, everything exquisitely quiet now. I propped up on my elbow, still facing Rob. The snow drifts around the car came half over the windows, encasing us in a Buick snow globe. I smiled at that idea. Far off on the horizon, a few scattered straw-colored rays gilded the top of Mount Quandary. Then I heard a chugging sound, which woke Rob minutes later as it came closer. He yawned, his eyes fluttering open, and a shiny yellow snowplow pulled to a stop beside us.

The plow driver climbed out, ran to my car, brushed the snow off the windows, and peeked in. "Anybody in here?" When he saw us in the back seat, he started kicking snow away from the door and pushing and banging on the handle. When it opened, he smiled. "Whew! You're Al Fortune's girl, aren't you? I know the car."

I nodded. "Yes, sir."

"You two got some worried-sick parents back in Juniper. How in the hell did you kids survive?" Then he noticed the Womb. "Somebody was using their head when they brought along that bag. It's twenty-five below out here. I had to go clear to Billings for another plow blade. Do you have enough gas to make it home?"

Rob nodded. "Yes, sir."

"Great." He smiled again. "There's one lane open all the way to Juniper." His beard was a bright orange red. "You two head north on it, and I'll head on to Casper."

+ + +

An hour and a half later, when we pulled to a stop in front of Rob's little white house with its smoking chimney, I was feeling both grateful and a bit in awe of him. I turned sideways in the passenger seat and studied him. Those boyish qualities that had always attracted me—the clean, masculine lines of his profile; his thick, dark lashes; and his cheeks, which always held a hint of color—were the same. But the set of his shoulders, the angle of his jaw, the grave look in his eyes—those were different. Rob was more a man than a boy now.

Was I more a woman than a girl? *Yes*, I thought. *I probably am.* BJ's death a year and a half ago had stolen the last of my innocence and precipitantly ended my childhood. Marooned in that snowstorm last night, I'd faced that loss with Rob and, in the process, forged a deep friendship. I knew as I stared at the strong, sad lines of his face that though we'd go our separate ways, we'd be irrevocably bound to each other by BJ and our sad, sad secret.

When Rob opened my car door to get out, I reached for his arm. Besides thanking him, there was one last thing that needed to be said. "It's not too late, you know, to stand up to Mr. Bonniface. You'd feel lots better if you did it. For yourself and for BJ. You have a right to know, Rob. Go out to the Bar Z, and don't leave till he tells you exactly what happened."

chapter twenty-three

JUNIPER, WYOMING

June 20, 1961

I t was Nella, what she'd said that morning after the snowstorm, that pushed me into this. Nella was why I was halfway to the Bar Z on the hottest day of the summer. I thought when she'd said it, she might be on to something. "It's not too late for you to stand up to Mr. Bonniface. Do it for yourself and for BJ."

Standing up for myself—for a long time, that hadn't seemed important at all. Just making myself keep going while the heart in my chest felt too beat up to work was the best I could do. Two weeks after BJ died, I was still suffering so bad I knew I had to do something different, so I decided to discipline my mind. Every time I thought about Beej, I made myself think about something else. There wasn't a goddamned thing I could do to help her now, anyway.

My mom—her heart was broken, too. She kept picking at me to talk to her about it. I don't think she believed the bee sting story, either. But, of course, if I'd talked to her, I'd have to start inventing lies. Because, shit, I still didn't know all of what had happened to Beej, either. All I knew was what hadn't—the bee sting.

Pork was the best person for me to hang with. Spring semester, our senior year in high school, that girl he was banging at work moved back to Texas, so he had time on his hands, too. He got me a summer job at the Creamery. So instead of working for Mr. Quackenbush, I made more money working with Pork, moving boxes and making deliveries. Plus, I got free ice cream. That was about my only good news last summer, free ice cream. On the weekends, Pork and me went to movies, played baseball, even tried a little saddle-bronc riding. I kept busy, kept the women—all the women—out of my life. That's how, somehow, I made it through the worst of it. Plus, I made it a point to tell anyone who tried to mention BJ that I was too damned sad to talk about her. Nella was the worst because she remembered BJ getting stung at Tomahawk Lake, so I dodged her whenever I saw her coming.

Going down to the university helped a lot. New coaches and classes, fraternity initiation, and football, football, football. My time down there got so filled up that I sometimes made it through a whole day without thinking about Beej.

But Nella was right. It was time for me to face up to Mr. Bonniface. Close the book. End the last chapter right, for Beej and for me, with the most understanding I could get. When Nella talked to me about it on the way home from spring break, I listened to her because Nella was well known for being smart.

And then I've thought a lot about how to do it these last six weeks of school. Man, I dreaded standing up to Mr. Bonniface. It was easy to put off as long as I was in Laramie. But when my freshman year was over, I'd still kept putting it off. Got myself back in the rhythm of the Creamery, all the while trying to get my courage built up. The more I thought about it, though, the more it seemed important to do. So I made a list on the back of a Creamery delivery sheet one day about points I'd like to say to Mr. Bonniface. Then I pictured how Coach Robbins—with his deep, slow voice—would talk about it. That was how I'd wanted to talk to Mr. Bonniface, in a dignified way like Coach.

Once I'd decided I was definitely going to do it, I started practicing out loud in the garage, where Mom couldn't hear me. I acted like my truck was Mr. Bonniface and went over and over, talking to my truck the way Coach Robbins would. That part was easy. The truck couldn't scowl at me or pound walls or kick things like Mr. Bonniface. Then, after all that practicing, I woke up this morning knowing that today was the day to do it. It was my day off. I was ready with what to say, and I'd talked to the truck enough to get down how I wanted to say it.

Me talking to Mr. Bonniface wasn't the only good idea Nella had given me that night in the snowstorm. She really helped me with some other important shit. Turns out, she wasn't a prick at all. And she didn't poke fun at me or think I was a baby when I cried that way over BJ. Nella really seemed to understand, and that helped. The biggest thing Nella convinced me of was that BJ dying wasn't just my fault only. I didn't understand how much I needed to talk about that. It's easier to face shit if you have someone to talk to. I'm not sorry I told Nella about the kid, either. It helped me, and it helped her, too. Made us closer. Nella won't tell.

I noticed I was gripping the steering wheel tighter the closer I got to the Bar Z. I remembered a World Series radio announcer sharing a Babe Ruth saying back when I was in the seventh grade: "It's hard to be a person that never gives up." And he was right. Damn hard. I gripped the steering wheel tighter. This time, I wasn't giving up till I got the whole truth about Beej. I wanted to know more than I was afraid of Mr. Bonniface. If he beat the hell out of me, at least I'd be able to look myself in the mirror and say I stood up to him. Jesus, though, I was scared shitless.

A daddy longlegs spider walked across my back last night. I was sleeping with my shirt off. Talk about something that gives you the creeps. As I got closer to the ranch, it felt like he was there again, back and forth between my shoulder blades.

Lloyd waved when I passed the gas station. At least it was a good-looking day, not a cloud in the sky. Seemed like every time I drove out to the Bar Z those last weeks before BJ died, it had been crappy weather.

My truck was running good. Pork stayed in Laramie over spring break just to work on it. A real friend. I liked rooming with him. He could fix anything. Even worked on the passenger-side door hinge Beej had hung on so much the door didn't close right. Hard to believe she'd died over a year and a half ago.

The sun was right overhead, so the mica on the flat side of Preacher's Rock glittered like gold. Fool's gold, they called it. I thought it was real when I was a kid.

I started getting snapshot pictures of BJ in my mind as I pulled into the canyon; the closer I got to the Bar Z, the more the pictures. That day by the creek, in her mom's yellow coat, when she was lit up by the funny sun. The deer and the God-feeling by the stream. Homecoming night in her bed, when we didn't have time, but it still was so great. And the last time I saw her, with her eyes so asleep she couldn't hardly talk. Little light halos around her there on the stoop. God, I was so glad the last thing I ever said to her was, "BJ, I love you better than anything."

It was the real thing with Beej and me. They called it puppy love in songs, but they are solid fucking-A wrong when it came to how we felt. Tears are so hard to hold back when you remember beautiful stuff.

What the hell did Mr. Bonniface do to her? I wiped my eyes and felt anger rise up in the back of my throat so strong that my jaws clenched and my teeth ground. The son of a bitch.

Then I was out of the canyon, passing the antelope at the old Franklin place, the Bonnifaces' first gate, rattling over their cattle guard. How do you make somebody tell you something when they don't ever want to see your ugly face again? Well, I was about to find out.

No sign of Mr. Bonniface in the hayfields along the road or by the barn. Or Mrs. Bonniface. Somebody at the flower shop told Mom last spring that Mrs. Bonniface didn't live in the big house anymore. I noticed the guesthouse up on the hill as I rounded the drive, red geraniums growing in the window boxes.

Mr. Bonniface's black Ford truck was sitting in the driveway in front of the big house. My throat went dry. Maybe the big house had been painted. It was the same color but looked cleaned up. The gate didn't squeak like it used to when I walked into the yard, then up the walk to the front stoop where I saw BJ the last time. I felt as home-sick for her then as the day she died. Was about to ring the doorbell when I saw the door was cracked open, so I stuck my head in and called, "Mr. Bonniface. It's Rob Hitchcock. Are you home?"

I pushed the door and walked in. Called again. No answer. The Remington was still there on the gun rack. The deer on the wall had both its eyes again. Something familiar caught my attention on a wooden dish under the gun. *Well, I'll be damned.* It was my buckeye. I walked over, picked it up, was rubbing my fingers over it when Mr. Bonniface and the dog showed up at the far end of the hall. I felt like a cowboy walking into the O.K. Corral.

"Who's there? Rob? I thought I heard you." His voice didn't actually sound pissed as he walked toward me. Angus shoved past him, ran up to me with his tail wagging. I scratched him behind his ears, was real glad to see Angus, but I didn't feel friendly to Mr. Bonniface at all. Was noticing everything about him. Either he was littler or I'd got bigger. He looked smaller.

When he got to me in the entry hall, he reached out to shake my hand. "Hello, Rob. Hadn't expected to see you here. How are you?" His eyes were looking me up and down. "We've been following your career at the university. You're making quite a name for yourself down there." His hair had turned white on both sides above his ears. His face was an unhealthy color, and the frown marks on his forehead looked like car ruts.

I realized I hadn't answered him. "Hi, Mr. Bonniface. I hope you're doing all right." I dropped the buckeye in my pocket and shook his hand. Reminded myself of my talks with the truck and lowered my voice like Coach. "I came out here to ask you to level with me, sir. I want you to tell me what really happened to BJ. I know for damn sure it wasn't a bee sting, because I saw your shot medicine in the icebox the day she died."

He looked surprised, turned away from me, put both hands over his face, and rubbed his forehead. "No small talk today, huh? Well, I give you high marks for directness." He raised his shoulders up toward his ears, then lowered them, like he was working something out of his back.

"No, sir. No small talk today. I was afraid to show up out here, Mr. Bonniface, but not coming has got me to feeling worse than coming. I loved her. I know you think I did wrong by getting her pregnant, but I sure loved the hell out of her. And I know one thing: if you'd-a let me marry her, she'd be here today." Surprised me, really, how calm I felt, how easy the words I'd said hundreds of times in my practices came out.

His forehead was sweaty. He reached into his pocket for his handkerchief and wiped it off. "We probably do have some talking to do. I've been through enough misery since she died that I sure as hell don't have any easy answers."

Angus and I followed him into the living room. The sun was streaming in on their big old piano. The candy dish Mrs. Bonniface kept on the coffee table was empty. I shouldn't eat candy, anyhow. I wanted to keep my mind on business.

"Sit down." He motioned me toward the sofa, and I sat. Angus stuck his rear end close and leaned into me while Mr. Bonniface walked back and forth across the room about three times, like he was trying to decide what to say. Then, instead of going to his own leather chair, he sat down on the sun-hot cushion next to me and put his hand on my shoulder. It felt like the spider moving under his fingers. I wanted to knock his hand off, but I didn't.

"I've missed seeing you," he said. "Missed BJ, missed Emily."

So Mrs. Bonniface *wasn't* in the house, and he thought I knew it.

"And you want the truth, the whole truth, and nothing but the truth?" He shook his head. He needed a haircut. "Well, I'm not surprised you're here. You have a right to know. In a strange way, son, you acted more the man than I did. I'll have to get your promise you won't tell another soul, Rob. Jack Justice—Doc—went way out on a limb to protect me."

I nodded to let him know that I promised.

He stood up, walked across the room again, his boot-heels clicking on the floor, then back, folded his arms, and looked down at me on the couch. "I was a medic, you know, in the war. It was easy to believe I could help her. I couldn't let her have a baby out of wedlock. It would have destroyed the reputation of my family, her chances for the future. Everything we stand for."

"But, Mr. Bonniface, remember? I *wanted* to marry her."

"I understand. Let me finish. I didn't *want* you to marry her. Call me a shortsighted, dumb bastard, but I believed I knew best. I have a drug that I use on my cows to strengthen their labor contractions. Sometimes to help them abort still-born calves. I told BJ about my idea—talked her into it, I guess. We were . . ." His voice caught in his throat like he was going to cry. "Very close, BJ and me."

My teeth clenched, and sweat had started pouring off my body.

"We went down to the barn so her mother wouldn't know." His voice was so regular and reasonable-sounding. "I made a pallet for her to rest on, carefully calculated her weight against the cow's weight, and cut the dosage proportionately. Then . . ." His eyes met mine, and he shook his head like he was so sorry. "I injected her with the drug, and we waited. At first, everything went as planned. She started cramping and bleeding, and the baby—a boy—was born quickly. But then the bleeding didn't stop, and nothing I did would slow it. It just got worse and worse." His eyes got wet with tears. He swallowed like it was hard for him to go on.

Something red—redder than a neon light, red—came into my head. I had to hold my clenched right fist down with my left so it wouldn't slug him. I hated him worse at that moment than I ever had my ole man. "Keep going, Mr. Bonniface." My voice still sounded in control, like Coach. "Tell me the rest. I hope you didn't leave her alone. Did she know you were killing her?"

He wiped his face again. "Of course I stayed with her—and no, she didn't think I was killing her!" His voice went high. "Jesus, Rob, I wasn't killing her. I was *helping* her. Helping you, too. Doing the best I knew how to get you both out of a tight spot. I have a phone in the barn. I called Doc the minute I realized things were going to shit, and he got there fast but just not fast enough." He stopped talking and stared at the floor. "There was nothing Doc could do." He closed his eyes and took a deep breath. "She just wouldn't stop bleeding. Finally, she lost consciousness, and then there was one last, massive hemorrhage."

"What about the baby, Mr. Bonniface. What happened to our boy?"

"He only lived a few minutes. He wasn't even as big as my hand, but perfectly formed. BJ wanted you to know that. She also said, 'Daddy, tell Rob I love him so.'" He choked like he hated saying it and began sobbing like a real baby.

Beej had to know she wasn't going to make it if she said that.

Something like barf or poison or fire from a dragon's mouth rose in my throat. I stood up, walked over to him, and slugged him. A solid hit to his lower jaw that splattered his sweat and glazed his eyes before he got a hand up to block it. He fell sideways, hit the coffee table, and dropped to the floor, still looking surprised. I wasn't through. I grabbed his shirt by the shoulders, ready to smash his face in, kick his teeth out, but I stopped myself. *I'm not my ole man. I don't have to settle things his way.*

Then my knees went. I slid down beside him, there between the coffee table and the couch. He was sobbing. I didn't want to slug him again. I just sat and watched him, couldn't bring myself to touch him, but I tried to say something good. "Mr. Bonniface, you didn't mean to do it." He was looking as sweaty, bloody, and miserable as a man could look, crying as hard as I ever wanted to see a grown man cry. Not me, though. I was just mad and goddamned disgusted. Coach had told me once you write your life story by how you behave. Well, Mr. Bonniface had written a fucked-up chapter when he did that to Beej, and he deserved to suffer.

Angus came over to him, started whining and licking his face. It seemed to bring him back. He sat up on the floor beside me. I saw I'd split open his lower lip. He pulled out his handkerchief and began mopping the blood. "Thanks for this," he said, wiping his mouth with his hand and smearing the blood on his cheek. "I've been wanting to slug myself for a long, long time. Are you through with me?"

When I nodded yes, he got up, stood for a minute—looking out at Mount Quandary—then went to sit in his leather chair. "You *need* to know the rest of the story, Rob. Because Jack Justice had to falsify BJ's death certificate, we took her straight to Billings and had her cremated. I knew you never understood that." He pointed at a big flowery glass jar on the mantelpiece. His voice dropped so low I could barely hear him. "We were destroying evidence, you see, so they couldn't charge him or me."

So BJ was their evidence they had to burn up, and all that is left of her is sitting up there in that jar on his mantelpiece.

I felt like I was going to barf. My fists clenched again; they couldn't help it. Angus came over and got in my lap on the floor. The action of rubbing his ears kept my angry fists from knocking the shit out of Mr. Bonniface all over again. I kept petting Angus, kept petting him, wouldn't let my hands stop petting him till I calmed down a little. I was reminding myself over and over that I was not my shit-faced, alcoholic ole man, that I could be different. But I had one last important thing I had to know. "Mr. Bonniface, what happened to our boy?"

He scowled. "Well, he was perfectly formed. God, I'd never want to go through that again—holding my own little grandson in my hands as I watched him finish dying." His voice broke. "Frankly, though, I'm not sure what happened to him after that. Things went all to hell with BJ, and by the time I got home from Billings, I had to look after Em as best I could. I pretty much left the barn and the cleanup to Buck. He did it all, and I've never discussed it with him."

When he said that, it felt like a rumbling volcano inside my head was about to blow until, for some reason, something Pork's dad said once popped into my head: "Never miss a good chance to shut up, boy." I think I remembered that just then because it was the right time for me to shut up and leave. Anything else I'd say would just make things worse, and Mr. Bonniface had answered all the questions I'd wanted to ask.

I gave Angus one last pat and got up, walked over to the leather chair, and stuck out my hand. "Mr. Bonniface, you may need a stitch or two in that lip. I think I'd better go. I didn't come out here to hurt you, sir, and I don't want something coming out of my mouth I'll be sorry about later. Good luck to you, Mr. Bonniface. I'm sorry I beat up your face."

"You know, Rob, BJ exercised better judgment than I knew when she chose you. You're a fine young man. I wish it could have ended different."

He didn't have any idea how much I still wanted to clock him. I just nodded and walked out the front door, feeling taller than when I had walked in. I thought about going to BJ's God-place on the river but didn't have the heart for it without her. So I climbed into the truck and headed for the front gate.

Just before the first cattle guard, I saw Standing Elk on top of the hill where the Bonnifaces have their family cemetery. He was waving his hand, motioning for me to come up. Shit! It was the last thing in the world I wanted to do, let the old Indian look through me one last time. But Beej would have wanted me to.

I turned off the truck, climbed out, and started walking up. Their cemetery is on the flat top of one hill, with another, bigger hill rising above it. Walking up the steep side, I couldn't see Standing Elk or the cemetery, but I started thinking about what Beej had said about him being her blood relative. BJ's grandfather must have had a child with Bird, Standing Elk's mother, long before Mr. Bonniface was born, because Standing Elk was lots older than Mr. Bonniface. That had to be the explanation. Which said to me that Standing Elk had as much right to be on the Bar Z as Mr. Bonniface did. I decided I'd ask Standing Elk if I was right about that, and also how had he known about our baby that day, once I got to the top of the hill. Five minutes later, when I made it, though, one of Standing Elk's crows was there, but the old Indian wasn't. Where was he? I got goose bumps.

The big crow wanted me to follow it. It stayed about a yard ahead of me, hopped a few steps, looked back at me, and hopped again. I followed it to a wooden slab marking Touser's grave—whatever dog that was—and then it flew to a new grave lower on the far edge of the hill. There was no grass on top of this one, and its marker was different from all the others. Not a big, polished headstone, but a fine sanded, carved wooden plank that was shiny and shellacked, probably with several coats. Baby Boy was all it said.

I felt a church-feeling as I knelt down and touched the letters so carefully carved into the wood. Somebody had gone to a lot of trouble to dig this little grave and make this special marker. I was sure it was Buck, and then Standing Elk had made it his business to lead me to it. God, I was glad for both of them, that our boy had a grave and a marker, and that I knew he would never be forgotten.

I stayed the rest of the afternoon up there in that cemetery. Though it was hot as blazes, I wanted to spend a little time with my boy and picture what he might have been like. I didn't see the crow or Standing Elk again, or any other person.

Nella had been right that I needed to stand up to Mr. Bonniface. Something inside me felt different now that I'd done that, a new feeling of confidence. I tried picturing in my head the kind of man that I could be. I wouldn't follow in my ole man's tracks; they weren't exactly the greatest footsteps to follow. And I wouldn't want to be a man like Mr. Bonniface. Rich as he was, he was right to call himself a dumb, shortsighted bastard. I really didn't look up to other important men like ole Gag-a-nee at Juniper High, either, with his little worm moustache, who seemed to actually enjoy disciplining students. Pork had experienced that more than once. Mean was not the kind of man I'd want to be.

The men I thought most of were kind, like Mr. Quackenbush with his turnips, and Carl, who bought me my first rubbers and took the time to teach me why to use them. And Buck, with his smashed-in, quiet face, who made that gravestone for our baby boy and buried him even though nobody else seemed to care. A man like Standing Elk, I could admire, too, the way he helped people when they didn't even know they needed it. As I looked down at the Bar Z spread below me, I decided that the only society-important man I respected was Coach Robbins, who really cared about his players, lived by his own life rules, and taught them to us. He stayed in shape, was there when we needed him. And he shut up unless there was something important to say. Like the time he was disgusted about my bruised shoulder but let it go. I decided I'd go back and thank Coach and ask him if we could stay in touch. If I ever found myself in another confused situation, he was the man I'd go talk to.

The cattle down below me were eating and mooing and humping each other, the way they always did. I was feeling calm now. My way forward, away from the Bar Z, seemed clear. Being a good man was more important to me than being a rich or a famous one. It felt great to get that sorted out.

I was also real thirsty. So I rubbed my buckeye shiny again, remembering homecoming night in BJ's bedroom, where I'd lost it. This definitely was the last time I'd come to the Bar Z. I had to put BJ behind me. Here, on the ranch, I was homesick for her in a way that was worse than having double pneumonia, which I knew about from having it once. Out there, I had a life and friends like Pork and Nella. Everything but BJ. Mr. Bonniface had said he was looking out for us with what he did—only I got my life back, and BJ lost hers.

Mom says that you learn good judgment from the mistakes you make using bad judgment. That makes sense to me. I should've fought harder for BJ, stood up to her dad way sooner. I should have put her first, no matter what. It didn't have to end this way. I'd sure as hell do it different now.

The orange sunset was making the top of Mount Quandary look like it was on fire. My last day at the Bar Z had come to an end. I pulled out my pocketknife and dug a little hole in front of my son's grave marker, dropped my buckeye in it for him, and covered it with dirt. Then I walked as fast as I could down the steep, gravelly hill, got in my truck, and headed down the rutty road back to my friends and football, my fraternity, and coaching classes, the life I would now live without BJ.

I didn't cry when I bumped over the loose cattle guard under the Bar Z sign for the last time. I just looked up and promised her I'd prove how much I loved her by the kind of man I was going to be.

Acknowledgments

I am so grateful for my mentor, the late PB Parris, and the members of our writing group who have "slodged" through this manuscript off and on for twenty-five years and given such tactful feedback: the late Elizabeth Daniels Squire, Virginia Sampson, Florence Wallin, Jan Harrow, Dr. Geraldine Powell, Bett Sanders, Nancy Hayes, Annice Brown and D.L Ellenburg, the best Beta Reader ever. This novel was my master's thesis project at the University of North Carolina at Asheville. Thanks to Dr. Ted Uldricks, the late Dr. Jeff Rackham, and Dr. Rick Chess. And I'm also a lucky duck because Kathy Meis and the folks at Bublish were the ones who encouraged me to exhume the manuscript and try again. A particular thanks to the ever patient Shilah LaCoe.

Since past is truly prologue, the heart of this book is Wyoming and my cherished childhood friends. I'm indebted to: Amanda Schiffer Kaufman, Cathy McDowell Ellis, Mary Orr Meyer, Allen Lee, the entire family of the late Torrey and Adrienne Johnson, and the late Jo Ann Wimer, tireless early editor and cheerleader.

Here in North Carolina, the encouragement of my friends has been vital. Thank you, Mary Hood Pearlman, Jasmin Gentling, Bunnie Burgin, Sheri Groce, Brucie Harry, Claire Talley, Sandy Holder, and the members of the No-Stress Book Club.

Several books were evocative as I tried to unearth those times past on a ranch. Most notable among them were *Breaking Clean* by Judy Blunt; *Leaning into the Wind: Women Write from the Heart of the West*, edited by Linda M. Hasselstrom, Gaydell Collier, and Nancy Curtis; and *The Cowboy Way: Seasons of a Montana Ranch* by David McCumber.

Finally, there's family. I've been blessed with such a great one. Thanks to our children, Brandon, Trent, and Kendal McDevitt. Travis, Tara, and Audrey Hinton, and Harper Beville, our grandchildren, have stretched my heartstrings and inspired me to persevere.

It is to my husband, an amazing person among all these amazing others, for whom I am most grateful. Thank you, Larry. Haven't we come such a marvelously long way together?

Made in the USA
Middletown, DE
16 May 2024